Last Call

A RED MOUNTAIN NOVELLA

Last Call

MARIPOSA
—BOOKS—

MICHELLE NAOMI MOSLEY

 Formatted with Vellum

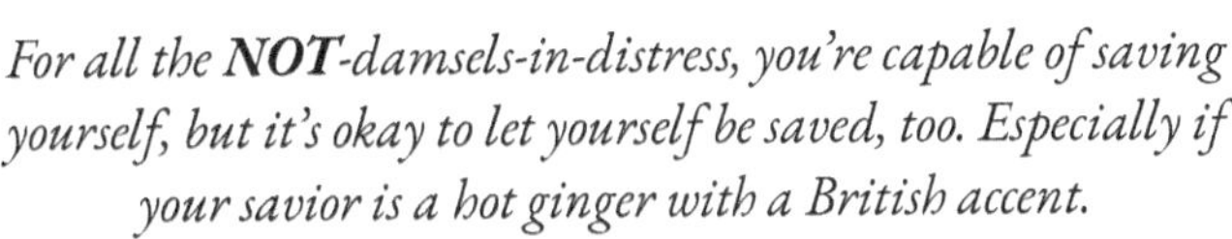

*For all the **NOT**-damsels-in-distress, you're capable of saving yourself, but it's okay to let yourself be saved, too. Especially if your savior is a hot ginger with a British accent.*

"You know I love a London boy...He likes my American smile."

— TAYLOR SWIFT, LONDON BOY

Author's Note

Dear Reader,

Last Call is a spin-off novella in the Red Mountain Series universe that can be read as a standalone, but does feature characters from the first book in the series, *Rare Blend*. If you'd prefer to avoid spoilers about those characters, I recommend reading *Rare Blend* first. However, it is not required to enjoy this story.

I didn't initially plan to write Hillary and Archie's story. At one point, while working on *Rare Blend,* I thought it might make a good short story or bonus chapter. But as more and more readers took a chance on *Rare Blend,* the interest in Hillary and Archie grew. So much so that their story sparked an idea and demanded to be told. I hope you'll enjoy returning to Red Mountain through a fresh perspective, with plenty of familiar faces, as well as flashbacks to London, where it all began.

While this story is mostly short and sweet, it does explore heavy themes of emotional, verbal, and physical abuse from a partner, including an on-page altercation. Your mental health matters to me, so please keep this in mind before reading.

This book is intended for adult audiences and contains sexually explicit content.

Please note there is content and situations within these pages that may be triggering to some. Some trigger warnings are spoilers for what's ahead, proceed at your own discretion.

- Domestic abuse (including emotional, verbal and physical abuse from a partner, not between MCs)
- Strong language
- Sexually explicit content
- Alcohol consumption
- Postpartum anxiety and body insecurity
- Mentions of derogatory American stereotypes
- Mentions of pregnancy (MCs)
- Mentions of trying to get pregnant (MCs)

Happy reading. Cheers!

Michelle

Playlist

Till Forever Falls Apart - Ashe & FINNEAS
London Boy - Taylor Swift
Fallingforyou - The 1975
Perfect - Ed Sheeran
End Game (feat. Ed Sheeran) - Taylor Swift
Adore You - Harry Styles
Cornelia Street - Taylor Swift
Lover - Taylor Swift
Ocean Eyes - Billie Eilish
Good Looking - Suki Waterhouse
Love The Hell Out Of You - Lewis Capaldi
Fade Into You - Royal Otis
About You - The 1975
Feels Like - Gracie Abrams
Hey Daddy (Daddy's Home) [feat. Plies] - Usher

About This Book

Hillary Hemingway is navigating the challenges of new motherhood, feeling as if the vibrant woman she once was has been overshadowed by the demands of parenting. When her best friend's birthday celebration in Red Mountain calls for her first weekend away from her baby, she's torn between the ache of separation and the prospect of much-needed time alone with her husband. As the weekend unfolds, the romantic getaway reignites the spark they shared before parenthood, stirring memories of how they first fell in love.

Archie Hemingway misses his wife, and when the chance to whisk her away for a weekend arises, he seizes it, hoping to remind her of their powerful connection—a love that bridged cultures and crossed oceans. Rediscovering each other, they dive into old memories, rekindling the fire that first brought them together.

A chance encounter became the start of an unexpected love story. Hillary's escape from a crumbling relationship in a foreign country led her to a pub where not even the last call was enough to keep her from falling for the irresistible bartender who would become her everything.

A weekend away. A love rekindled. Sometimes, finding each other again is just the beginning.

CHAPTER 1

Hillary

HOT VACATION SEX

Now

"I can't leave her," I tell my husband Archie as I clutch onto our six-month-old daughter. Josephine squirms, but I still hold her firmly against my chest, inhaling her baby smell and wishing time would freeze. Every day she gets bigger and every day I mourn the baby I'm losing while simultaneously celebrating the person she's becoming. It's a mind warp to both hate and love the growth of your own child.

"Hillary, we're only going to be gone two nights. She'll be fine." Archie rubs my back, trying to comfort me, but all it does is make me want to cry. "Mum will take good care of her, and she'll be perfectly comfortable staying home, sleeping in her bassinet. It will be familiar to her."

Of course, I know all of this, but it doesn't stop me from panicking at the thought of being apart from her. Since giving birth, I haven't been away from her for more than a few hours, and even that nearly drove me insane. But I also know Archie and I severely need some alone time, some time when we're not mommy and daddy. I can't remember the last time I did a full beat of makeup or dressed in something that didn't have an elastic waistband. I'm so far from the woman he met, I'm not sure how Archie finds me attractive right now.

He looks at me, tears brimming in my eyes, and wraps his arms around us. "I'm sorry," I choke out. "I told myself I wouldn't be this kind of mother. I said I wouldn't let myself go or lose myself. I'm such a hypocrite."

Childless me sure had a lot of opinions on motherhood before karma made me eat my words.

"Stop being so hard on yourself. These feelings are normal. I don't want to leave her either, but I know it's healthy if we get away for the weekend without her. And the only reason I'm okay with it is because I trust Mum and she's aware of the routine we have with her. She'll be leaving to go back to London at the end of the month, so we need to take advantage of her still being here to help."

I nod against his chest. Everything he's saying is true. We've been so lucky Joanna has been able to help. She's been staying with us since we brought Josephine home from the hospital, and it's been amazing. It's been a wonderful surprise, considering how much Joanna disapproved of me when Archie and I first got together. We were able to build a relationship before Archie and I got married, but there was a time when I thought we would never get to the place we are now.

"You're right, you're completely right." I slide Jojo to my hip and wipe under my eyes. I need to pull it together. I used to be the kind of woman who took charge and looked good doing it. Now I'm crying with spit up on my two-day-old sweater, not having showered in three days. I'm a wreck, a disgusting wreck.

"Here," I pass Jojo off to Archie. "I'm going to shower."

He grabs her with ease, and she settles against him, clutching his shirt with her little fist. She's a total daddy's girl.

"Want some company?" Archie asks suggestively, raising his brows.

I snort, gesturing my hand up and down my body. "Babe, I need to take an everything shower before you can see me. I'm not cute."

He walks over to me and leans down to kiss my forehead. "You're sexy as hell. And tonight, when we get to the inn, I'm going to ravish you."

My stomach tightens as heat spreads across my chest. We've had fairly regular sex since I got the all-clear. At first it was a timid re-exploration, unsure of how to be with each other after the hurricane that is childbirth. Now that we've got the hang of it, it's been very quick, very let's-both-orgasm-and-go-to-sleep. We haven't had the good stuff since before Josephine was born and I desperately, desperately need the good stuff.

He grabs my chin with his free hand and plants a possessive kiss on my lips. For a moment I forget where we are and how I look, and slip my tongue in. He groans, deepening the kiss. It isn't until Jojo starts gabbing in her adorable baby voice that we pull apart, both dazed.

Archie clears his throat and adjusts Josephine. "When you're ready, we'll head off."

Inside the shower, I get straight to work, shaving every inch of my body and deep conditioning my unruly curly hair before running a wide-tooth comb through it. Not only am I trying to look good for my husband, I also haven't seen my best friend Marisa in months. I'd prefer to not look like I'm totally falling apart. She wouldn't judge me, but the nurturer in her would worry, and I don't want the weekend to be about me.

Ethan, her boyfriend, and the only man I would ever approve of for her, invited us to come celebrate her birthday weekend in Red Mountain. While I miss having her live nearby, watching her be as happy and in love as she is makes the distance completely worth it.

He was kind enough to set us up in a suite at a local inn, while he and Marisa stay in a suite across the hall, making it a bit of a staycation for them.

Despite having some major separation anxiety, I'm extremely excited to spend the weekend drinking wine and catching up with my bestie, and hopefully having some hot vacation sex with my husband.

CHAPTER 2

Archie

MY LITTLE AMERICAN

Now

"How is she?" my mum asks while making a bottle.

"Stressed, worried, anxious, all the above."

"Understandable. A mother hates to be away from her child, even when she needs it." She comes up to me and grabs Josephine out of my arms. "You're an adult, and I still have a hard time thinking of you living so far away. In America, of all places." She breathes a laugh and gives Jojo a belly scratch. "Isn't that right, my sweet girl? My little American."

I laugh, shaking my head at her. "Interesting coming from the woman with a suitcase filled with food from Trader Joe's."

She huffs. "The store is brilliant. I'm going to start a petition to get one back home, honestly. Whoever invented that cookie butter deserves a medal."

"We'll be sure to bring some when we visit at Christmastime."

Mum leans Josephine back in her arms and starts feeding her the bottle. Josephine clutches it, holding it with a firm grip. She's only recently started to hold her own bottle, and you'd have thought she performed magic when Hillary and I witnessed it for the first time.

"We're going to have some proper Gran and Jojo time this weekend. I need to get in all the cuddles and kisses before I head off. You two have a good time, and don't you worry about a thing. I raised three kids—I know what I'm doing. You can trust me."

"We both trust you. That's not the issue. We're nervous parents."

She wipes some milk that's dribbled on Josephine's cheek and sways her softly back and forth. "I'll check in multiple times a day and send proof of life pictures. You two need some alone time. To rest and recharge."

Truer words have never been spoken. We need this time together—*I* need time with Hillary. I miss my wife. Parenthood has consumed our lives, and while I wouldn't change a thing and love our daughter more than life itself, I sometimes feel like we're losing little pieces of us in the day-to-day chaos. Between work, life obligations, bedtime routines, and barely any sleep, it's easy to forget what it felt like when it was just us —when our days were filled with long conversations and lazy Sundays in bed. I want that back, even if it's just for the weekend.

After loading up our suitcases, I run through Hillary's checklist while I wait for her to come downstairs. Ever the type-A, she's got Josephine scheduled down into ten-minute increments. Hillary only breastfed for three months, so thankfully that's one less thing to worry about. I set all the supplies on the counter. Mum knows where everything is, but it'll make Hillary feel better to see it laid out.

When Hillary finally comes down, her eyes are lit with excitement, but the tight press of her lips reveals a hint of worry. She glances toward Mum holding Josephine before her gaze meets mine, brows knit, forming that adorable crease between them. Despite how uneasy I know she feels, I can't help but take notice of how fucking beautiful she looks. Her wild curls flow freely, swaying at her shoulders, and she's put on an expert-level of makeup, where I know it's there but have no idea what's been applied. She's wearing denim shorts and a tucked in black T-shirt with sandals that show off her bright pink polish. Her hips flare where the belt cinches her waist and my fingers twitch, begging to touch her, to run my hands along her newer curves. It's been ages since I've seen her look how she does now. There's never a moment that I don't find Hillary to be the most beautiful woman I've ever laid eyes on, but seeing her dressed up and glowing from finally taking some time to herself, she's all the more beautiful. I knew she needed this. I knew she needed a reason to pamper herself.

"She's all set, love," I reassure her, giving her a warm smile. "Everything's set out just how you like it."

Hillary lets out a breath, nodding. "I know, I know. It's just...the first time leaving her. Feels strange."

Mum glances up with a playful grin, bouncing Josephine gently. "You're only going to be gone a couple days. And if anything happens, I'll be in touch straightaway. Go on now, both of you. No more dilly-dallying."

When Hillary reaches Mum and Josephine, she leans over, brushing her hand gently across Jojo's cheek. Josephine's tiny fingers open and close around the bottle, her eyes half-lidded, already drifting off in Mum's arms.

"Goodbye, baby girl," Hillary whispers, her voice thick with emotion. She presses a soft kiss to Josephine's forehead and smooths back her curly red tendrils. "Be good for Gran, alright? Mommy and Daddy will be back soon."

Mum gives Hillary a reassuring smile. "She's going to be just fine. We'll have the best time, won't we, Jojo?" Mum coos, swaying her softly, and Josephine lets out a tiny sigh, snuggling deeper into Mum's embrace.

Hillary nods, blinking back the tears threatening to spill over. She looks at me with red, glassy eyes, and I give her a gentle nod, letting her know it's okay.

For a long moment she remains unmoving, and my heart stills as I hold out my hand, hoping she doesn't suddenly back out of our plans. She takes it, squeezing just a little tighter than usual, and I can feel the tension easing out of her shoulders as she does. We share a quick glance back at Mum and Josephine—Jojo's eyes starting to flutter shut as she drinks. It makes me feel a little easier, seeing her safe, content, and in Mum's arms.

In the car, as I start the engine, Hillary sighs and leans her head back against the seat. "You think she'll be alright? I get that we're already going, but..." She breaks off and looks back at our house, a war of emotions flashing across her face. I knew it was going to be hard, but now even *I'm* second-guessing whether or not we should leave. Maybe this is too soon, maybe she's not ready.

With a steadying breath, I look between my wife and our home and decide to be the stronger one. If we don't get away now, there's no telling when we'll get the opportunity again. And the more time that passes, the more likely Hillary is to continue to fade away.

"She's in excellent hands," I say, reaching over to intertwine our fingers, letting my thumb soothingly rub over her knuckles. "And tonight, we're going to have some much needed alone time." My implication is obvious, and the burning gaze I give her confirms my intentions.

Hillary's lips lift into a faint smile, and the worry in her eyes softens, replaced by a flicker of heat. It's a tiny victory, but a victory all the same. Tonight, for the first time in a long time, it'll just be me and my wife.

CHAPTER 3

Hillary

LIKE A SNACK

Now

The car is quiet as we pull out of the driveway. I stare straight ahead, trying to ignore the uncomfortable twist in my stomach. Archie glances over, lifting our joined hands to place a gentle kiss to my palm.

"She'll be okay, love," he says softly, like he's trying to coax me into relaxing. "We'll be back before she even notices we're gone."

He's so patient with me. Always. Sometimes, it feels like I'm still waiting for a dark side of his personality to emerge, and I continue to be shocked by his unwavering goodness.

I try to settle back in my seat, watching as Seattle's sunny July sky shines brightly down on us as we drive away from the city. I want to be excited; Archie and I haven't had time alone in what feels like forever. But there's this persistent guilt tugging at me, like a little voice admonishing me for being the kind of mother who leaves her baby for something as frivolous as a weekend of wine tasting. I feel like a bad mom, as illogical as it sounds.

"You're overthinking it," Archie says, glancing at me with that knowing smirk.

"Am I that obvious?"

He laughs. "Only to me. I've always been able to read you like a book."

Despite myself, I smile, letting out a breath. He has a way of doing this—of making me feel like I'm on solid ground, even when I feel like I'm sinking. From the moment we met in that dark London pub, he saw me—the real me. He saved me from my asshole boyfriend at the time, but more importantly, he saved me from myself. He made me feel alive in a way I didn't know I needed.

"You know," I say, glancing over at him. "The first thing I noticed about you when I walked into your brother's pub was your red hair. I couldn't tear my eyes off the hot ginger working behind the bar." I run my hand through his hair, letting my nails scratch against his scalp, eliciting a moan.

"Oh, really?" He raises an eyebrow, keeping his gaze on the road but clearly amused. "Should I feel objectified?" he teases. "I did catch you staring, love. Subtly is not your strong suit."

"Good thing I wasn't trying to be subtle."

He chuckles, casting me a sidelong glance. "Neither was I. And had the circumstances been different, I probably would've hit on you."

"I think everything happened just the way it was supposed to."

"I couldn't agree more."

The knot in my stomach eases just a little. Archie knows how to pull me out of my head and back into the moment. Sometimes I forget, with all the exhaustion and routines of life now, that we were those people once—the ones who took risks, stayed up all night talking, changed our lives for each other.

"I was thinking," he says, turning onto the main road. "Maybe we could take the scenic route."

"The scenic route?" I give him a look. "Is that code for 'we're about to get lost?'"

His grin widens. "Only if you want it to be. Thought we could take White Pass instead of Snoqualmie Pass, take the long way, take in the views, enjoy the journey."

"Oh, sure, the views," I cross my arms. "This wouldn't be a ploy to feel me up while you drive, would it?"

He laughs, giving my knee a slow squeeze. "Well, you do look like, what is it the kids say these days? Like a snack?"

I snort and roll my eyes even though my stomach flutters at his compliment. It felt good to get dressed up and ready, already I feel more like the woman I remember I used to be. The truth is, I don't mind a little detour; I like the alone time.

And what is it about a man driving that's so attractive? Archie puts his hand on the back of my seat as he reverses out of the gas station and my stomach dips as I watch him the whole time.

He pulls onto the highway, resting his hand on my thigh and rubbing softly. It's an innocent touch, but the pulse building between my thighs feels anything but innocent. I glance over at him, taking in his sharp jaw, the red stubble dotting his cheeks and jawline. He's usually clean-shaven but I love when he has a little stubble, the bits of dark auburn emphasize his red hair, adding a touch of ruggedness to his chiseled features. It's hard to believe we've only been married a little less than a year and a half and before that we dated only a year before getting married. Once we realized we were it for each other, nothing was going to get in the way of our happily ever after. Not distance, or citizenship, or cultural differences. Somehow, we made it work. He's still the same man I met when the last thing I was looking for was love. A man who saved me—a stranger—from an unhinged boyfriend. Little did I know he would become my everything. So much more than I could have ever imagined.

CHAPTER 4

Hillary

A "ROMANTIC" GETAWAY

THEN

"Get your ass back in this car right now! I'm not messing around, Hillary!"

"Get fucked, Kyle!" I yell, not bothering to turn back and face him. He's been a total asshole from the moment we started this vacation, but he's especially worse after he's been drinking. If he thinks I'm getting in a car with him behind the wheel when he's this drunk, he's got another thing coming.

The problem is I have no idea where we are, and it's already dark. London is feeling as foreign as Russia despite the non-existent language barrier. I was so excited about what was supposed to be a dream vacation I didn't bother to check the crime rates of any of our destinations. So far, I've survived Spain and France, but I'm completely naïve to England's crime rate and for some reason can only imagine a Jack the Ripper-like criminal emerging from the shadows as I pass through the dimly lit street. It's late and all the storefronts are dark and closed. I have no plan here, my only thought is to get as far away from Kyle as possible.

I know my plan is failing though, because I can hear him stomping behind me. His huffing and puffing sounding closer and closer despite me picking up my pace. I don't want to seem dramatic, but his behavior has been escalating—escalating to the point I no longer feel safe with him. Last night he drunkenly shoved me, pushed me onto the bed and pressed his body over mine. Nothing happened, because he quickly passed out, but I know where he was heading. I know what could've happened, and that's when I realized I needed to put an end to this hellish vacation. I stayed up all night trying to figure out my next move. Unfortunately, all that did was leave me tired and my senses dulled as we went about our day today, one where I pretended everything was okay so I wouldn't set him off. He was fine until dinner. Two drinks later and back was the man I've come to fear.

I turn down an alleyway, hoping to lose him, without realizing what a stupid move it is on my part. There could very well be an unhinged person waiting to attack, or a drug user who might hurt me. This situation is a nightmare, one I'm not sure how to wake up from. One thing I know for certain is that I need to get the fuck away from Kyle before his verbal threats turn physical and he makes good on his intentions from last night.

The only comfort I can cling to is the weather. It reminds me of Seattle, when it's not quite raining but there's a mist in the air that dampens your skin. It feels nice. It feels like the only thing keeping me sane as I search for something that's open so I can hide out.

In the distance a blue flash of light catches my attention. My heart skips, and I cling to the hope that it's an open business. At this point I'm not exactly picky. I nearly jog to get to it and thankfully cutting through the alley has gotten me far enough away from Kyle that I no longer feel his presence behind me. As I get closer, the sound of music drifts out into the street and I realize it's a pub. Relief floods me. It's not a sanctuary by any means, but it feels as close as I'm going to get to one and it's the perfect place to sit and hide out while I come up with a plan.

When I look back over my shoulder once more, Kyle is nowhere to be found, so I step into the darkened pub. Warmth envelops me like a soft blanket after the chill of the evening. The rustic wooden beams and cozy nooks beckon, pulling me away from the chaos infiltrating my mind. I keep imagining Kyle's face on every face I land on, as if he's everywhere, but I know logically it's my mind playing tricks on me.

I likely look a bit crazed at the moment, which would explain the strange looks being shot my way. That and my curly hair is probably a frizzy mess from all the humidity.

A bitter laugh escapes me, and I shake my head, dismissing the frustration that has been clawing at me since Kyle and I left our hotel. I'm a stupid woman for getting myself in this situation to begin with. I'm smarter than this. I know better than to let a man have this much power over me. But then again, maybe I'm not so smart, because I got away from him for now, but I'll have to go back at some point to get my things. This might be my most poorly executed plan to date.

As my eyes take in the small pub, it seems every seat and table are occupied, leaving me no choice but to head for the bar.

The polished wood gleaming under the warm lights casts a glow around it. Behind the bar stands a red-headed man. He's leaned over the counter with an easy smile resting on his face as he chats with a beautiful woman sitting in the barstool across from him. She must have said something funny because he laughs and throws a rag over his shoulder, nodding at her as he makes a cocktail. I claim the only open barstool and dig out my phone. Unsurprisingly, I have ten missed calls from Kyle and even more unopened texts. There are a few texts from Marisa. I'm ignoring them for now. I feel guilty about it, but if she knew how badly this trip has gone, she'd be on the next flight over, no doubt maxing out a credit card. She has enough money problems; I don't need to add to them.

A throat clears, forcing my eyes off my phone and to the bartender in front of me. Up close, he's even more handsome. My skin flushes, heat creeping up my neck as his gaze lingers on me expectantly.

I'm literally running from a man, the last thing I should be doing is checking out another one in the process.

"What can I get you?" the bartender asks, his voice a low rumble that manages to dull the noisy atmosphere of the pub.

My eyes meet his light blue ones, and I'm caught off guard by the tenderness in his expression, like he can tell I'm going through it. Or I ust look that awful and he feels bad for me. It's likely the latter.

"What do you recommend?" I ask, trying to keep my voice steady. In truth, my mind can't think of anything to drink besides water, and I could use something a lot stronger than water.

His eyes narrow thoughtfully. "Long day, I take it?"

"You have no idea." A rueful smile tugs at my lips.

"Alright," he says, nodding as if he already understands more than he's letting on. "How about something smooth? We've got a lovely red from up north. Or maybe you'd like a whiskey to chase away the chill?"

"Whiskey sounds perfect."

He nods, turning away to retrieve a glass, his movements steady and practiced. As he pours, I study him. He's dressed a lot more formally than I would expect for a place like this, wearing black slacks that look like they've been tailored to fit him and a button-down with the sleeves rolled to his elbows. His hair looks like it started the morning off perfectly in place and has since fallen out of form, pieces swaying over his forehead and skimming his brows. He flicks his wrist, checking his watch, and I try my best to not stare at his corded arms as he continues maneuvering around. When he sets the glass in front of me, he doesn't step back immediately, lingering with an unhurried calm.

"You're American," he says, his voice curious rather than judgmental.

"Did my accent give me away?" I laugh, taking a sip. The warmth of the whiskey spreads through me instantly, taking some of the day's tension with it.

"Just a bit." He grins, leaning slightly against the bar. "What brings you all the way here?"

"A *romantic* getaway." The sarcasm in my voice isn't lost on him.

His brows lift. "Sounds...unforgettable." His lips twitch in amusement as he looks on either side of me. I'm clearly alone.

I let out a breathy laugh. "Not exactly the word I'd use."

He looks as if he's about to say something, but a call from down the bar interrupts. "Archie, when you're ready!"

Archie. The name suits him, though I can't explain why. With a quick, apologetic smile, he nods. "Duty calls. But don't go anywhere—last call isn't for a while yet."

As he moves away, I take another sip, feeling oddly disappointed he's left. The whiskey's warmth lingers, but it's his easy smile and kind eyes that stay with me even as he works his way down the bar, his attention shifting between customers.

The front door chimes and my head quickly whips to the entrance. A relieved sigh releases when I realize it's not Kyle. I probably shouldn't keep my back turned, in case he manages to sneak in here unnoticed, so I pivot in my stool and watch the door, occasionally taking a sip of whiskey.

After some time, I scan the room, noticing a group of locals huddled together in laughter, while a couple is engrossed in a deep conversation at the far end. My heart sinks a little as reality starts to set back in. I have no idea what I'm going to do, and the selfish part of me wonders how everyone can just go about their lives as normal while mine crumbles. I want to call my mom or Marisa, but I'm embarrassed. I talked up Kyle so much, when really, I had no idea who he truly was. Now I'm going to have to explain that he's actually a monster and I was too blind to see the obvious signs. He's the one in the wrong yet I'm the one embarrassed. This whole thing is so fucked.

My attention returns to Archie. Strangely, he seems to be the only thing strong enough to distract my mind from racing out of control. He's pouring drinks with an ease that makes it look effortless, and my breath hitches in my throat as I watch his biceps flex under the linen of his shirt. The corners of his eyes crease as he laughs and chats with the patrons with a level of familiarity that makes it seem like I'm intruding on a family gathering. I should direct my focus on my dire predicament, but I can't seem to tear my eyes off him. He looks up, catching my gaze, and the corners of his mouth lift into a charming smile. He caught me checking him out and my cheeks heat as I cast my eyes downward, fixating on my half-full glass. I've never had any strong opinions on gingers, but this one in particular is doing it for me. This must be my coping mechanism; checking out a hot stranger to distract from my angry boyfriend that will no doubt find me soon.

I look at the door again. No one has come through it for a while but it's only a matter of time before he finds me. Kyle isn't the kind of man who gives up. It's one of the characteristics that drew me to him in the first place.

"Last call for drinks!" Archie shouts, his voice deep and inviting, cutting through the chatter of the pub. I glance at the clock. It's already later than I thought, almost midnight, and my stomach turns at the thought of Kyle waiting for me outside, still stewing in his erratic anger. My plan of hiding out here is obviously flawed since I have nowhere to go once it closes. The hotel Kyle and I are staying at is not an option.

Archie approaches, taking a glance at my glass. "Would you like another?"

I really should try to stay somewhat sober, so my mind is clear when I have to face Kyle, but I also need some liquid courage.

"One more. The same."

He nods and works at pouring me another drink.

As he slides the glass over to me, his eyes catch mine and a question flickers in them.

"It's none of my business, but do you have a way to get back to wherever you're staying? Would you like me to call you a car?"

My chest sinks, my worrying pulse picking up speed. "That won't be necessary," I say with a tight smile.

His eyes pinch. "You do have somewhere to go, correct?"

Can this man read my mind? I rear my head back, caught off guard by his questioning. "Why would you ask me that?" I end on a wheezing laugh, feigning nonchalance.

He shrugs easily but his eyes regard me with concern. "American girl far from any tourist traps, alone, and glancing at the door every five minutes with worry. I guess you could say I've been paying attention, and what I've concluded is that you're in trouble."

I take a slow sip of whiskey. "I didn't realize you were also a detective." My lips quirk up in a smirk, an attempt at flirting to keep the conversation light.

His expression is unamused. "Engineer actually. This is my brother's pub, and he was short staffed." He nods to the man serving drinks to a big group. "Will is shit at finding good employees. Loves to take in strays who lack any sense of responsibility."

For brothers, the two couldn't look more different. Archie is tall, fair skinned, with red hair and his brother is shorter, with a stocky build and jet-black hair.

"Takes after my mum's side," Archie provides, apparently watching my eyes compare the two.

"It's nice of you to help him."

His shoulders lift, and he glances up at the ceiling. "He lets me stay in the flat upstairs for free. It's the least I could do."

"Sounds very generous of him. Do you like living above a bar—or pub, I mean?"

He smiles at my self-correction. "For now. The company I work for moved me to the head office so I needed to find a place closer to the city. It's a bit crowded, though, since my sister Emma stays when she has class at university."

My brows raise. "So, all three of you are sharing that space?" The pub isn't necessarily small, but I can't imagine the space above it is large enough to be comfortable for more than a person or two.

Archie laughs, shaking his head. "No, Will lives with his wife, Sarah."

"Still, two can be a crowd."

He nods, agreeing with me, his eyes never leaving mine. He let me divert the conversation, but it seems the diversion is over.

"Are you going to tell me what's going on, or will I have to pull the truth out with more whiskey?"

Despite recent events suggesting otherwise, I'm a pretty

cautious woman. I lock my car doors as soon as I'm inside. I don't get gas at night. I don't shop with earbuds in. I listen to true crime podcasts and watch murder documentaries to stay up to date on the latest tactics of criminals. I'm not the kind of woman to trust a stranger, but I find myself wanting to spill everything to Archie. To divulge all that's transpired with Kyle. Maybe if I voice it, I won't feel so dramatic anymore. Maybe I'll feel validated. He's given me no reason to trust him, but I find I'm trusting him more than I probably should.

"I'm on vacation with, my...boyfriend, I guess..." Boyfriend feels like the wrong word, but that's what he is. Not for long, though. "We've been traveling across Europe, celebrating the sale of an app he developed. It was great at first, but I'm starting to realize there's a lot I didn't know about him, and that maybe he's not the guy he's been portraying himself to be."

My eyes look away, shame wrapping around my neck and climbing to my face.

Archie's expression twists. "Has he hurt you?" His voice is raspy and strained.

I shake my head, biting my lip to keep hold of my emotions. "Not physically. He—he gets a little mean when he drinks. I'm probably blowing things out of proportion. I'm feeling homesick and I think it's making me emotional and overdramatic."

"Don't do that." Archie's eyes hold mine captive. "Don't try to explain away his behavior and make excuses for him. There's a reason your instincts brought you here and away from him. You should trust them."

I'm quiet for a moment. "Thank you," I say with a nod before taking a big gulp of whiskey, letting the liquid push down the lump that's lodged in my throat.

His brows lift, and he shakes his head. "Sorry." He chuckles, some of the thickness in the air dissolving. "I didn't mean to get so intense on you. I'm Archie, by the way." He extends his hand across the bar to me and I instinctively reach out for it, letting his large, warm hand envelop mine.

"Hillary," I tell him as we shake.

"Hillary," he echoes, as if he's testing out how my name falls from his lips. He smiles softly. "Very nice to meet you, Hillary."

CHAPTER 5

Archie

HERE TO ESCAPE

Now

The drive from Seattle was only four hours, but with a mix of dry, desert air and being away from our little one, it's like we've entered a different world once the Welcome to Red Mountain sign comes into view.

"Hillary, love. Time to wake up." I give Hillary a light shoulder shake as we pull into the inn's gravel drive. She doesn't usually fall asleep during car rides, or nap at all, but as soon as we started crossing the mountains she passed out. A pang of guilt hit me the instant I heard her soft snoring. She's obviously exhausted. Maybe I haven't been pulling my weight as well as I thought I had.

Hillary's eyes come awake and sparkle with excitement as she takes in the vineyard-clad hills rolling across the horizon. Even though this is technically Marisa's weekend, I can tell Hillary is ready for a small escape of her own.

"Look at this place," she breathes, leaning forward to peer out the window. "It's like something out of a painting. No wonder Marisa didn't want to leave—hell, we just got here, and *I* don't want to leave."

It really is beautiful, rustic and inviting, with a cozy charm that feels perfectly tucked away from the rest of the world. The inn is set back among rows of grapevines and surrounded by gardens that spill over with lavender and sage. A small wooden sign swinging on a post by the front door reads *The Vintage Inn.*

"Ready to be properly spoiled?" I grin, shutting off the car.

Hillary turns to me, her eyes dancing. "Yes, please."

I hop out, and as I grab our bags from the back, I glance over to see Hillary stretching her legs, her blonde curls catching in the light. She's got this glow to her, despite the bit of hesitancy lingering in her posture. I know it took all her resolve to leave Jojo with Mum, but we're here now—and hopefully, we can both relax a bit.

As we make our way to the front lobby, a warm breeze drifts by, carrying the scent of ripe grapes and a hint of oak from the nearby wine barrels. I reach for her hand, giving it a reassuring squeeze. "Here's to our first night alone in...what? Seven months?"

"Not even that." She laughs, a touch apprehensive. "I'm not sure how to do this anymore. What do married couples do when it's just the two of them?"

I laugh, nudging her shoulder. "I think we'll manage."

Based on the photographs Ethan sent me, he booked us a lovely suite. The plan is to wine taste for most of the day tomorrow. But tonight? Tonight, I plan to remind my wife how well we fit together. How explosive our chemistry is. How what we have was worth moving thousands of miles away from the only home I'd ever known, because from the moment her green eyes landed on mine, she became my home.

"Tonight, it's just you and me, and room service, no interruptions."

Hillary blushes, and there's a hint of eagerness there, too.

The woman at the front desk checks us in with a cheerful smile, hands us the key, and gives us a quick overview of the property. "And if you'd like a bottle of our house cabernet sent up, just give the front desk a call."

I thank her, and we make our way to our room—a suite that overlooks the vines stretching toward Red Mountain, the town's namesake. It's stunning and tranquil, exactly what we both need.

As I close the door behind us, Hillary lets out a sigh, kicking off her sandals and padding over to the bed. She collapses onto it with a contented groan, her eyes closed and a slight smile on her lips.

"Alright, then?" I ask, setting our bags down and joining her on the edge of the bed.

"More than alright," she replies, her eyes still closed, but her hand reaches out, grabbing hold of mine.

"All alone," she says softly, looking up at me. "Just the two of us."

"And here's to it," I murmur, leaning down to kiss her the way I've been waiting to since we left. I slide my tongue in, and she welcomes it, opening up more for me and curling hers against mine. I groan and grab hold of her jaw, feeling the need to claim her mouth like this is our first time. It's been far too long, and I moan against her lips, feverishly devouring all of her at once.

She pulls away, and her hooded eyes look at me as her lips hover over mine, soft and familiar, yet electric after all these months of stolen moments and half-finished conversations. She tilts her head up to kiss me, roughly, more frantic. Melting into the kiss, her fingers tangling in my hair as if we're making up for lost time.

I move my lips to her jaw, and work my way down, placing open-mouthed kisses down her neck. She smells intoxicating, like coconut and spring florals, and I want to bury my face in her neck just to inhale her.

"Maybe a few days away isn't such a bad idea after all," she sighs, barely above a whisper.

"Glad to hear it," I reply, rougher than I intended.

I start to pull at her shirt, needing to free her of all clothing right this instant. I hadn't intended to attack her the second we got a few minutes alone in the suite, but I can't help myself.

She must feel the same way because her hands claw at my clothing just as determined as I feel.

Once her top is off and her bra is revealed, I nearly drool as I drink in the sight of her. It doesn't matter how many times I've had her, she's never stopped rendering me speechless.

I reach out to cup her breasts and she groans, curving into my touch. Once I'm able to free one, I bend my neck to capture it in my mouth.

She lets out a trembling breath. "Sorry they're not as perky as they used to be."

I pause, pulling my mouth away to meet her gaze. "Why on Earth would you worry about that?"

Her skin turns pinkish as her eyes focus on the light pouring through the windows. And then it hits me—it's the daylight. Since Josephine was born, we've only ever had sex in the safety of our dark bedroom with no time to spare and no light for exploration. She's worried about how I'll view her changed body.

"Hillary," I say firmly, so she knows I'm being serious. "Your body is a fucking dream. The fact that it grew our daughter only makes me want you more. In fact, let me put another baby in you right now so I can prove to you how badly I want you."

My mouth returns to her neck as my cock hardens at the thought of getting her pregnant again. She was insatiable during pregnancy, and some possessive, animalistic part of me enjoyed every second of it. I loved watching her fuller body ride me to her heart's desire. Watching her breasts double in size and bounce as we fucked; it was sexy as hell. I still picture it when I jerk my cock.

Her hands push against my chest, forcing me back.

"Slow down there, mister." She laughs. "There will be no baby making this weekend. I'm back on the pill, remember? I need at least a year, maybe more."

"Fine," I groan and suck the soft skin under her jaw. "But my cock is still filling your pussy up completely." I start working at her shorts. "I want to be leaking out of you all weekend."

Her response is a high-pitched exhale, and I take it as a yes.

Together we remove her shorts and the remainder of my clothes, the only piece of clothing on her is her pulled down bra, which I promptly unclasp and throw across the room.

"Oh, fuck, love. You have no idea how badly I want you."

She scoots to lie at the head of the bed and spreads her legs open for me. "Please fuck me, Arch."

Fuck, I love her.

Without hesitation, I skip the foreplay and go straight for her pussy, lining my cock up at her entrance, and rubbing the head between her seam to test how wet she is for me. She's fucking soaked and I relish in the feeling of it completely sheathing me. Despite not having properly played with her pussy to warm her up for me, her body is so used to my size, that I slide right in, filling her to the hilt. Her warm, wet pussy grips me like a vise. I plan to make love to her in every which way all weekend, but right now I'm fucking her hard and rough until she can't think.

Her legs wind around me as my hips rock into her. Her full tits bounce to the rhythm I set. I love this side of her, the sensual woman that emerges outside the walls of her demure image.

Soon my orgasm releases, and at the same time, Hillary's pussy pulses around my cock, her waves of pleasure drawing the cum right out of me.

We stay like that, wrapped in each other, the soft rising and falling of her chest against my arms, completely content. It's funny how just having her here—without schedules, without interruptions—makes me feel like the man I was when we met, daring and reckless, ready to fall all over her.

But then her stomach rumbles, loud enough to break the moment, and we both burst out laughing.

"Starved for sex and food, I see." I chuckle as I pull away.

Hillary grins, sitting up and running her fingers through her hair. "Well, in my defense, we didn't stop for anything, not even coffee, on the way here."

"Let's fix that." I grab the room service menu from the bedside table and slide it over to her. "Pick your choice, love. Anything you want."

She glances over the options, her eyes lighting up as she spots the local specialties. "Ooh, how about this? The charcuterie board with a fresh baguette, smoked salmon, and that cabernet they mentioned downstairs."

"Sounds perfect." I press the button on the room phone.

While I order, Hillary wanders over to the window, wrapped in a sheet, to look out over the vineyard. She seems lighter, like the weight she carries every day has lifted, and it makes me feel both guilty and happy at the same time. The setting sun casts warm streaks of light across the room, turning the vines golden and filling the air with a soft, hazy glow.

Once I'm off the phone, I move to stand beside her. "Beautiful view."

She nods, her gaze on the endless rows of grapes below, mine focused on her, tracing the way the sun catches her profile as she takes it all in. I'll never know what I did in another life to be deserving of spending the rest of this one with her, but if this is the universe's idea of a reward, I'm starting to think I might've been a saint—or a really charming criminal.

"It is. I can see why people come here to escape."

I slip an arm around her waist, pulling her close. "I'm glad we made it."

She turns to me, her hand resting on my chest. "Is it weird that I feel guilty for enjoying the quietness? I didn't even check in with your mom when we got here, some mother I am," she huffs, shaking her head.

I inhale deeply, wondering if I'm ever going to be able to take her mind off motherhood long enough for her to truly enjoy herself. "I texted her when we got here, and she said all is well."

She stiffens but doesn't move away. "Oh...okay. Thank you."

"You need to relax." I pull her closer until her head rests against my shoulder.

Before long, there's a knock at the door, and I step away to let the server in as Hillary slips into the bathroom to change. He rolls in a tray set with our charcuterie board, wine, and fresh-baked bread. After he leaves, Hillary reemerges in a robe and her eyes widen as she takes in the spread, practically bouncing in place with excitement.

We settle down at the small table by the window, the view of the vineyards before us. I pour us each a glass of the cabernet, rich and deep, and raise mine in a toast.

"To us," I say.

She clinks her glass against mine, her smile soft. "To us."

We sit in comfortable silence, sharing bites of smoked

salmon and cheese, sipping the wine and savoring this rare alone time.

Eventually, Hillary puts her glass down and leans back, her eyes drifting over to me. "I'm sorry for being such a downer and not as fun as I'm sure you were hoping for. Do you think I'll ever get better at this?"

I reach for her hand across the table, lacing my fingers with hers. "It's okay to not be okay. Right now, my only concern is getting you to relax. And we don't have to do weekends away for some alone time. Maybe a date night or two a month would be a good thing to incorporate."

She nods, a small, hopeful smile on her face. "I'd like that."

The wine is nearly finished, the light outside slowly fading to dusk. Hillary takes my hand and drags me to the velvet-plush couch that looks out toward the view. Once I'm seated, she crawls in my lap and curls around me as we watch the last traces of sunlight dip behind the hills. The stars begin to make their appearance, one by one, like tiny pinpricks of light breaking through the dark.

Cuddled up, I'm reminded of everything that brought us here. The laughter, the quiet moments, the easy silence that only comes with time and trust. It's all still there, even if we had to steal away from our regular lives to find it again.

And in this quiet, stolen moment, I feel that sense of peace I'd almost forgotten we could have, the peace neither one of us knew we needed until we found it in each other.

CHAPTER 6

Archie

FUCK OFF, WEASLEY

T**HEN**

The door to the pub swings open, letting in a blast of cold night air, and I catch sight of him before she does. Her boyfriend—if you can even call him that. I know it's him instantly—call it good instincts or just that he has an American arrogance about him that makes it all the more likely. I can't help the way my hands curl into fists at my sides. I've seen his type before. The swagger, the cocky tilt of his head. Men like him walk in thinking they own the place, only to find they don't. Not here, not tonight.

He's muttering under his breath, his jaw tight as he scans the room. His eyes land on Hillary, who's sitting at the bar clutching the whiskey I just poured her. She looks relaxed for the first time all night and the air leaves my lungs as my body tenses. I have a very bad feeling this exchange isn't going to go well.

Hillary hasn't noticed him yet; she's too wrapped up in the safety of her drink, her shoulders finally loosened. For once, she's not glancing over her shoulder, not bracing herself.

But then he calls her name, loud enough to turn a few heads.

"Hillary!"

She jumps, her spine going rigid again as she turns and winces. There's a flash of fear in her eyes before she masks it, and that's enough for me to maintain my wariness.

He marches over, his eyes darting to me, sizing me up before he focuses back on her. "What the hell are you doing in here? Did you really think I wouldn't find you?"

"Just...warming up." Her voice is small, apologetic. I hate it. As if she's had to shrink herself to appease him.

He steps closer, and some of my restraint snaps. "Is there a problem here, mate?"

He barely looks at me, dismissing me with a wave of his hand. "No problem at all, *mate.*" I fight an eye roll at his attempt to mock my accent. "Just grabbing my girlfriend and getting out of here. Car's ready."

I don't budge and neither does Hillary. "She looks comfortable where she is."

He finally shifts his focus fully onto me, his eyes narrowing. "And who exactly are you?"

"Just a man serving drinks." I give him a once-over, letting him see I'm not going to back down. "And one who's not going to let you harass my lovely customer."

Hillary glances between us, looking torn, like she's not sure what to say or do. She opens her mouth to speak, but he cuts in before she can get a word out.

"This isn't any of your business, alright?" He turns back to her. "Let's go, Hillary."

But she hesitates, her eyes darting to mine, and in that second, I see it—the silent plea for me to intervene. Her breath quickens, rising and falling far too quickly. She's terrified of him.

"You're not taking her anywhere." My voice is low but

clear. If he wants her, he's going to have to go through me. And unlike him, I have an entire bar full of rowdy, inebriated men who wouldn't hesitate to back me up.

Her boyfriend's face darkens, and he steps forward like he's about to make some sort of scene. But I hold my ground, arms crossed, my gaze steady on him.

"We're closing soon." I glance over his shoulder, making eye contact with Will. "You're leaving, she's staying."

His face hardens, but he doesn't move. "What's your deal, huh? Trying to play the hero?"

"Not really," I reply, keeping my voice even. "I don't know how men act where you're from, but around here, we don't scream at our women. And we certainly aren't about to let you think your behavior is acceptable in this establishment. Leave on your own or leave with some *assistance*. The choice is yours."

He sneers, looking from me to Hillary. "Fine. You want to stay here with this guy, Hillary? Slum it with the help. Go ahead. But don't expect me to come back for you when you change your mind."

There's a pause, and for a moment, I worry she'll give in, follow him out of some sense of obligation or fear. But then she straightens, her stare steady on him.

"I think I'll stay," she says only slightly above a whisper but strong enough to make her point.

He shakes his head, muttering something under his breath as he turns on his heel and storms out. The door swings shut behind him, and the pub settles back into its usual hum.

I let out the air I'd been holding in my chest and turn back to Hillary. She looks shaken, her hands wrapped tightly around her glass, but a small, watery smile pulls at the corner of her lips.

"You didn't have to do that," she murmurs, looking up at me. "I don't know—"

Our moment of peace is short-lived, because just as quickly as he left, Hillary's menacing boyfriend reappears, bursting through the door once again.

He races up to Hillary and roughly grabs her hand, forcing her arm to extend out unnaturally.

"No, you know what?! No. You are not going to act like a spoiled little bitch and think you can walk away from me."

She yelps as he drags her to stand, and it's enough of a commotion for the pub to go dead quiet and take notice of what's happening.

This is a small neighborhood pub, filled with regulars and plenty of familiar faces. Hillary stood out the moment she walked in, but paired with this menace of a man, she has the attention of everyone in here. And we don't take kindly to a man mistreating a woman.

Will's eyes meet mine from across the room and a silent conversation passes between us. We tend to be underestimated and dismissed due to our friendly demeanors but get alone with either of us in a ring and we aren't quite so friendly. We've both been boxing since we were kids, and Will has gotten in his fair share of brawls well before owning the pub. This arrogant piece of shit is going to have to get through a mob of angry Brits if he thinks he's walking out of here with Hillary against her will.

"Let go of me, Kyle," Hillary grits, trying to pull her arm out of his hold.

"You're being an ungrateful bitch. Do you realize how much money I've spent on you, and this is how you repay me?"

He starts dragging her to the door and Will casually stands in front of it, crossing his arms.

I roll up my sleeves even more, flexing my hand open before setting it into a firm fist. I didn't expect to get into a fight today, but it seems to be the direction we're heading.

I'm not sure what it is about her, but I could sense she was in trouble from the second I spoke to her. And for reasons I can't fully wrap my mind around, I feel an odd urge to protect her. Maybe it's her angelic face and that beautiful, blonde mermaid hair, or maybe it's something else. Whatever it is, I can't simply stand by and watch this arsehole mistreat her.

He keeps trying to drag Hillary toward the door, but she holds her stance and shoves off him, attempting, again to get out of his grasp.

"I believe she said to let her go."

"Hey, fuck off Weasley."

Jesus Christ. Real original. Like I've never heard that one before.

By now, every man in the pub is either standing or half-standing, ready to insert themselves. Will raises his hand, palm out, to the guys, telling them to hold off.

Hillary twists and just when I think she's going to get free, so I can pummel this fucker to the ground, he spins her back and slaps her across the face.

The sound echoes like a crack of thunder, followed by her shrieking gasp.

My head shakes, and my eyes blink several times. All noise dulls like my head is in a dense fog. There's no way I just saw that; my mind must have imagined it. It had to. My body is reacting before my brain can make sense of things, and I'm leaping over the bar and barreling toward the man. He sees me coming, and in a split-second releases his hold on Hillary. With her safely out of the way, I tackle him to the ground and get one good punch in, right on the jaw.

And fuck does it hurt. I haven't been in a real physical fight in a very long time, and I forgot how much it hurts to truly punch someone. Just as I'm about to get in a second one, Will is yanking me off, and Elliot and Toby, two regulars, are clutching onto Kyle on either side.

Will holds me back and whispers in my ear. "As my silent partner, I'm going to beg you to not finish this fight. Let the guys handle him."

I nod, breathing deeply, feeling the red haze of my anger slowly dissipate. Elliot and Toby chuckle as they haul Kyle out the door. They're more than happy to have an excuse to hit something. I lose interest in him the moment he's no longer my problem and my eyes scan for Hillary. When they finally land on her, she's being comforted by Sage, Elliot's wife and somewhat of a mother-figure to the misfits who frequent the pub. My sister Emma is also standing by her. She must've heard the commotion and made her way downstairs.

Hillary's red-rimmed green eyes meet mine. She mouths *thank you* and her silent words break through my chest. So much has happened in a short span of time, and all I can think of is making sure this beautiful stranger is okay. And maybe I'm also thinking that I wish she wasn't a stranger at all, because every part of me wants nothing more than to wrap my arms around her and bury my nose in that beautiful, curly hair.

CHAPTER 7

Hillary

MASCULINE PROWESS

Now

Sunlight filters through the inn's gauzy curtains, casting a golden hue over the room as my eyes adjust. Next to me, Archie's already awake, his hair tousled and an easy smile resting at his lips as he watches me.

"Mornin', sleepyhead," he murmurs, brushing a curl off from my forehead.

Yawning, I stretch out against the plush bed. "Good morning," I reply, voice still groggy. The scent of coffee wafts through the open window, along with a hint of warm desert air, the hot sun heating my exposed skin. "I could get used to mornings like this."

"Thought you'd enjoy sleeping in a little," he says, sitting up and throwing on a shirt. "But I have to warn you—Ethan roped me into playing a round of pickleball before the wine tasting starts, so we have to be downstairs soon. No lazy morning, I'm afraid."

I can't help but laugh. "Pickleball? Really? What is it with men and pickleball?"

"We have to show off our masculine prowess." He smirks. "Don't worry; I'll make it look good." He leans down and presses a quick kiss to my lips before hopping off the bed.

I grin as I watch him get ready, feeling a surge of excitement for the day ahead. Not only do I get to explore Red Mountain's wineries, but I'll finally see Marisa again. It's been months, and while we talk constantly and FaceTime, nothing beats catching up in person.

I get ready alongside Archie, choosing a sundress since it's supposed to be almost one-hundred degrees today. Even in the summertime, Seattle rarely gets over ninety so it'll be an adjustment.

By the time we make our way to the inn's breakfast nook, Marisa's already there, nursing a coffee and giving me an excited wave. She looks effortlessly chic, as always, in a sundress nearly identical to mine. We've always had this issue, unintentionally dressing alike.

"Hillary!" She squeals and pulls me into a tight hug the moment I reach her. Despite being shorter than me, she lifts me off the ground and a huff of air escapes me. "I can't believe how long we've gone without seeing each other!"

"Way too long," I agree as she sets me back down.

"Look at you!" Her eyes track me from head to toe. "Of course your body bounced right back."

My cheeks flush. I may look like I'm back down to my previous weight, but my body feels anything but back to normal.

Ethan extends his hand out to me, but I bypass it and force him into a side hug. He stiffens, allowing it, and I bite my lip to keep from laughing. One thing about me is I'm a hugger. As long as he's keeping my best friend happy and glowing, he's going to get a hug from me. If he fucks up, then she can call me to help her bury the body. Until then, it's all hugs.

We settle into our seats, and I notice Marisa's eyes dart

toward Archie and Ethan, who are already discussing all things pickleball. We share an eye roll and giggle. I love that they get along, and if we have to suffer through pickleball talk, then so be it.

A waitress comes by and fills the empty coffee mugs at the table while taking our orders. Marisa reminds me to order a hearty meal to handle all the wine we'll be consuming, so I take her advice and order biscuits and gravy.

Archie leans over, whispering something to Ethan, and they both laugh, looking like two teenagers planning a prank. I'm glad to see Marisa has loosened Ethan up enough to laugh and look relaxed, a far cry from the man she used to vent to me on the phone about when she first arrived in Red Mountain.

Marisa catches my eye and raises an eyebrow. "They're really into this, aren't they?"

"Oh, you have no idea." I chuckle. "Apparently, they're planning to 'wow us with their masculine prowess.'"

She snorts, stirring her coffee. "This should be good."

After breakfast, we make our way to the inn's small recreational court. The guys left ten minutes before us and are already warming up, paddles in hand. Archie tosses the ball to Ethan, who catches it with a flourish and winks at Marisa from across the court.

"Prepare to be amazed, baby," Ethan calls out, and Marisa blushes like a school girl.

"Kick his ass, Arch," I shout, exchanging a grin with Marisa. We settle onto a nearby bench, eager spectators as they begin their game.

Archie serves first, a look of intense concentration on his face as he whips the paddle across his body. The ball zips toward Ethan, who barely manages to return it, and the rally begins. They're quick, light on their feet, and surprisingly competitive—each trying to outplay the other with spins and tricky shots.

Marisa leans in, voice low. "This is strangely attractive, isn't it?"

I laugh, nodding. "I know, right? I don't think I've ever found pickleball so sexy. Must be all the grunting."

We sit there, cheering them on as they play and catch up on life. She tells me all about the house her and Ethan are building and the progress they've made. She talks about wanto to get married one day, and I can tell she's nervous about broaching the subject. Little does she know, Ethan already has a ring, and I helped pick it out. I'm not the best secret keeper, but I'm absolutely keeping it to myself. I don't want to spoil their special moment. I show her pictures of Josephine, and she's amazed at how much she's grown in the three months it's been since she's seen her.

"Look at her chubby little legs. I just want to eat her!"

I shove my phone away. "Please don't eat my daughter. It would make things weird."

She laughs and steals my phone out of my hand, continuing to swipe. "I'm not going to come across some nude picture you sent Archie, am I?"

Snorting, I sneak a look at Archie. He's sweating, causing his red hair to appear more auburn. His T-shirt hugs against his chest, stretching deliciously across it. I suck in my bottom lip, blatantly checking out my husband. "No, but he might get one later."

Time flies way too quickly and soon the sound of the ball bouncing against paddles comes to a stop. The game ends with Archie and Ethan both panting, and grinning widely. Ethan won, but they both look triumphant. They walk over, shoulders heaving, and collapse onto the bench beside us, their competitive energy still lingering in the air.

"Told you we'd impress." Archie winks at me.

"Oh, absolutely," I reply, trying to keep a straight face. "I'm blown away by your skills."

Marisa snickers, nudging Ethan. "Guess all that practice paid off, huh?"

Ethan rolls his eyes, but there's a hint of pride in his smile. "I can't help how competitive I get. It's a curse of my DNA."

After a quick freshen-up back at the inn, we head out to the first winery—Ethan's family winery of course. Ledger Estate Winery and Vineyards is an elegant chateau-like estate surrounded by rolling vineyards that stretch as far as the eye can see. The main building is made of stone, with black iron detail and ivy trailing up the walls. A sprawling patio looks out over the valley, lined with wrought iron bistro tables. It's beautiful, timeless.

Inside, the tasting room gives a European vibe with black-and-white marble flooring and intricately carved stonework with wood craftsmanship along the walls. A hostess greets us with a friendly smile, despite her widened eyes and shaking hands as soon as she notices Ethan. She leads us to a table on the patio and hands us a tasting menu that's nearly as long as a novel.

"Will that be everything, Mr. Ledger?" she asks nervously.

"That's all, Gwen, thank you. Make sure Rae is our attendant."

She nods and scurries off while Archie and I look over the options.

We're barely half-way down the list when our attendant arrives at the table. An older woman with hints of gray streaked through her dark hair and deep lines at the corners of her eyes. "Welcome to Ledger, I'm Rae," she says, her tone friendly and inviting. "We'll be starting with some of our signature whites today. If you'd like, I can guide you through each tasting, or you're welcome to explore on your own." She looks to Ethan for guidance.

"Starting off with whites sounds great," Ethan tells her.

She smiles tightly and heads back inside.

Archie slides an arm around my shoulders and glances at Ethan. "You must rule with an iron fist. Got the whole staff shaking in their boots."

Marisa lightly smacks Ethan's chest. "We're working on him being friendlier. It's taking a while for them to warm up to him."

Ethan shrugs, clearly not as worried about it as Marisa is. Marisa grins, looping her arm through Ethan's. "I'm just so happy you guys were able to make it. I'm sure it's hard to get away now that you have Josephine."

I've been trying to not be *that* mom and check in every five minutes, but after pickleball I sent a text to Joanna and she was kind enough to send me tons of pictures. Josephine was all smiles, which then made me feel an odd sense of jealousy. I love that Jojo is a happy baby who does well with her gran and other family members, but I also get hit with wanting to be the only one she smiles and giggles for. There are so many things all the books prepare you for, all the advice friends have, but that feeling wasn't one of them. Archie must sense me tense because he gently rubs my back, bringing me out of my rabbit hole of worries.

"It was tough, but it's good to get away. Maybe next time we'll bring her, make it a family trip," Archie chimes in, giving me a moment.

Marisa nods eagerly. "Oh, yes! Hopefully the house will be done by then and you guys can stay over."

Rae returns with a bottle. "This is our Sauvignon Blanc," she says as she pours Marisa's glass. "Crisp and light, with notes of green apple and citrus. Perfect for a sunny afternoon."

She finishes pouring and explains she'll be back shortly to fill our glasses for the next tasting.

I take a sip, letting the flavors linger on my tongue. The cool, refreshing taste of the wine is bright and tangy, and it instantly lifts my mood.

"Oh, that's good," I murmur, glancing at Archie. His eyes are closed as he tastes, savoring it like he's analyzing every single note. He's always analyzing, his engineer brain never quite shutting off.

"Not bad," he says, eyes traveling over me. "Have I told you how stunning you look in that dress?" His gaze drinks me in as he smirks in a way that tells me he's picturing me naked.

My cheeks heat as I shake my head at him. It's been a while since I've worn a dress, let alone one this revealing, and I don't mind his appreciation one bit.

He leans over to whisper in my ear. "It's going to look even better on the floor when I peel you out of it later."

A giggle bubbles out of me, both from his suggestive words and the tickle of his breath on my neck. He's not usually so flirty with me in public. If this is his method to distract me, it's working.

It's working so well I have to squeeze my thighs together to relieve the building ache, but it does nothing to alleviate me.

We move on to the next glass, a Chardonnay with hints of pear and vanilla, and then to a rich, buttery Viognier. Each wine seems better than the last, and soon me and Marisa are laughing and comparing our very amateur tasting notes, which turn into a mix of half-baked metaphors and absurd comparisons.

"This one tastes like...crème brûlée and a new pair of Louboutins. Definitely expensive." I hold up my glass, laughing a little too hard at something that isn't nearly as funny to anyone but us. The wine giggles have officially taken over.

"Really? I was getting hints of Jell-O," Marisa adds, chuckling. "Creme brûlée could never be Jell-O."

We bust up laughing and the guys look at us like we've lost our minds, clearly not getting our reference to *My Best Friend's Wedding*.

"Are we sure we're not wine critics?" My lips curve up as I raise my glass. "We might have a future in this."

Ethan snorts. "If wine critics rate everything based on women's shoes and obscure movie references, then yes, you've found your calling."

"And dessert," I retort. "Can't forget the dessert."

"Don't you think I'm hilarious?" Marisa asks Ethan.

A hint of a smile crosses his face. "Yes, baby. You're hilarious, as always."

Satisfied with his answer she leans into him and gives him a light peck on the cheek, to which he smiles and tucks a strand of her hair behind her ear.

They're so adorable it's annoying. Annoying and wonderful. After her tool of an ex, she definitely deserves some happiness.

As the tasting continues, the conversation flows easily as we catch up on life. We talk about everything from Marisa's latest projects at *The Vine*, the small magazine she runs that's associated with her dad's newspaper, to my emerging return to work. I'm only going back part-time, starting next month, but it's still stressful to think about. Ethan and Archie can't seem to let go of their pickleball game and keep talking about it. Luckily, Marisa and I have plenty to discuss, and tune them out.

When we get to the reds, things start to get a bit hazier... drunker. Our attendant brings out a Malbec with deep berry flavors and hints of spice.

"Now, this is where I could get in trouble," Marisa murmurs to me as she swirls the glass. "Something about red wine makes me want to do bad things." She looks at Ethan, and their stare is so heated I'm surprised their clothes haven't disintegrated right off.

I turn away, feeling like I'm intruding on them, and focus on Archie.

"I actually don't know what red wine does to me. I'm more of a whiskey girl."

He smirks, the gleam in his eyes sending a flutter through me. "I'm aware, love. I guess we'll find out tonight just how naughty some red wine can make you."

It's a playful remark, but the intention threaded through his words makes my cheeks flush. Averting my gaze, I try not to smile too obviously. Out of the corner of my eye, I notice Marisa catching the exchange and raising her brows with a knowing grin.

"Having fun?" she asks, her voice overly suggestive.

As I'm about to say something, a shout has my head whipping back.

A few tables over, a couple is looking to have an intense conversation as a tipped over bottle of wine spills across their table and drips down through the decorative holes of their bistro table.

"You're always so fucking clumsy!" the man yells at the woman.

She frantically pats her napkin on the table. "Maybe if you weren't such an asshole, Kyle, I wouldn't have knocked over the bottle!"

Archie's gaze locks with mine. It's funny how just hearing a name can send you back in time.

CHAPTER 8

Hillary

DON'T BE DAFT

THEN

I'm still trying to catch my breath as the pub settles into a dull whir, people glancing at me and murmuring, but pretending they're not. My cheeks sting, one more than the other, and the adrenaline buzzing through my veins has started to wear thin, leaving me unsteady and hollow.

"Fuckity fuck, what the fuck just happened?" a young, red-headed girl to my right says.

"Em!" the older woman in front of me chastises. "You're going to scare the poor girl."

"Please, Sage. Like I'm scarier than a man." The girl scoffs.

"I'm Emma, by the way." She points to the older woman. "That's Sage." Emma wraps an arm around my shoulder as if we're close friends. "Seems like you've had an exciting evening."

I freeze, completely caught off guard by her over-friendly demeanor.

"I usually don't come down here because drunken idiots give me hives," Emma continues. "But then I heard all this ruckus and couldn't help but check it out. I can't recall the last time I saw my brother get into a fist fight. Must've been when he was still in secondary school—"

"Em," Sage interrupts. "You're talking her ear off."

Emma, unfazed, continues chattering away but I only catch about every other word, my mind spinning. Something about writing a paper and her brother's pub and something else. I can't seem to follow the conversation.

She guides me to a chair, partially hidden by the bar. Emma's arm is warm and steady around my shoulders as she deposits me onto it. Beside her, Sage is nodding along, regarding at me with a knowing look that's somehow both comforting and a little intimidating. She's one of those women who seems like she's been around long enough to see it all, and I have a feeling nothing shocks her anymore.

"Here, hon," Sage says, handing me a glass of water and tearing the whiskey glass I didn't realize I was still holding out of my clutches. "Sip on this. You're looking a bit pale."

I take the glass, nodding mutely, feeling the cool edge of it against my palm as I try to settle my vibrating nerves. I can still feel the pressure of Kyle's hand on my face, see the anger in his eyes. How did I let myself get here?

"Don't you worry about him," Sage says softly, as if she can read my mind. "The likes of that man aren't worth a second thought. Not when you've got good people around you now."

"Exactly," Emma squeezes my shoulder. "You don't have to deal with him anymore tonight. My brothers made sure of it."

Her words sink in slowly, and my chest loosens, if only a little.

"Thank you," I manage, my voice embarrassingly shaky. "I...I don't know where I'll go tonight, but I'll figure it out. I don't—"

"Oh, don't be daft!" Emma's tone leaves no room for argument. "You heard Archie. There's no way we're letting you go out there on your own after that. You'll stay with us, right upstairs. It's nothing fancy, but you'll be safe, and that's what matters."

I glance at her, surprised by her kindness. She barely knows me, and yet here she is, offering me a place to stay, a slice of safety.

"Really?" My voice is small, the relief and exhaustion fighting for dominance. I know Archie told Kyle that I was staying, but I didn't think that was him inviting me to actually stay in his flat. Was it?

"I wouldn't want to impose..."

My protest is weak, but it might be all that's left of my pride.

"It's not imposing." Emma waves off my concern with a grin. "Besides, I think Archie would have my head if I let you wander off into the night after all that." Her smile fades, and she shakes her head. "That bloke has some nerve."

Sage huffs, her arms crossed. "Well, he's gone now, and that's what's important."

I give a weak smile. "Thank you, both of you. Really."

Emma squeezes my shoulder. "Come on. Let's get you upstairs." She looks back at Sage. "You'll keep an eye on things down here?" The crowd is back to buzzing, hyped up from the commotion. Both Archie and Will look frazzled as they manage it all.

Sage smirks. "Darling, I practically run this place. Archie and Will can thank me later."

Emma gives her a little salute then steers me toward the door that leads to the stairs. It's narrow and dark, and my body feels heavy as I follow her up, my steps a little unsteady. By the time we reach the landing, my mind is starting to clear, the reality of everything sinking in.

Emma leads me to a cozy living room, full of mismatched furniture. The scent of old wood and something faintly floral permeates the air. It's warm, familiar, and comforting in a way I haven't felt in a long time.

"Toilet's just down the hall, and I'll set you up in my room tonight," she says, flicking on a soft light. "I'll sleep on the sofa, it's no trouble."

"Oh, you don't have to—" I start, but she dismisses me.

"Please, it's the least I can do. Plus, you look like you could use some rest."

I nod, unable to argue. Emma exits the room to grab some bedding, and I sink down onto the couch, exhaustion hitting me like a wave. I don't know what comes next, but for tonight, I feel something I haven't felt since this awful vacation began —safe.

CHAPTER 9

Archie

PUNISH ME, DADDY

Now

"Today was fun," I tell Hillary as we get settled into our suite for the evening.

"It really was." She flops onto the bed with a silly smile. I haven't seen that smile in quite some time. "I think I'm a little drunk." She giggles and then hiccups.

I join her on the bed, desperate to be near her and touch her creamy, soft skin. "You're never allowed to get rid of this dress."

She laughs. "It'll go out of fashion soon. Everything does eventually."

I play with the tied strap on her shoulder. "Don't care. It stays."

The way she's lying has her breasts spilling over the neckline of the dress, practically begging to be fondled. This dress has been torturing me all day, and the only thing keeping me sane was imagining taking it off of her, strap by strap, tie by tie.

A trembling sigh floats between her lips as I lightly brush

my thumb over the swell of her breasts. "You wore this on purpose. You enjoy driving me mad, don't you, love?"

She nods sucking in her bottom lip and shooting me her impossibly large green eyes. "Maybe."

I dip my head, grazing my nose against her neck and letting my lips linger over the delicate skin. "Such a bad girl," I whisper.

She shivers and tips her head back. "Punish me, daddy. Show me what a bad girl I've been."

She started calling me daddy when she was pregnant, and fuck if it didn't completely ruin me. Even now, my cock goes from a growing erection to hard as a rock.

Any resolve I had is long gone, banished by alcohol and Hillary's filthy little mouth. A mouth that looks like it could use a mouthful of my cock right about now.

Standing, I turn Hillary, situating her neck so her head hangs off the bed. She's familiar with what I'm doing and lets me position her just the way I like.

This bed is as high off the ground as our bed back home, the ideal height to fuck that pretty little mouth of hers.

I unzip my pants and my cock springs free as she opens her mouth for me in a perfect O, so eager to please.

I start slow, letting my cock fill her mouth gently, allowing time for her throat to loosen.

The corners of her eyes begin to water as she takes me deeper, and it's such a beautiful sight. My gorgeous wife with so much of my cock in her mouth I can see it bobbing in her throat, not a gag reflex to be seen.

"Touch yourself while I fuck your face. I want that pussy good and ready for me to fill once I'm done with your mouth."

She obeys me, dipping two fingers inside her panties and rubbing at her clit. Moisture darkens the light-pink cotton, causing my cock to ache to be inside her.

Hillary likes control, but when it comes to sex, I'm the one in control. With me she doesn't think, she just feels. And I make sure it always feels really fucking good.

She moans, the vibration crawling up her throat, and my balls tighten, so close to spilling in her mouth.

"Take off the panties, I want to see you."

She gives me a garbled *mm-hmm* and quickly has them off with her dress hiked up and her legs spread.

"Now show me how wet you are."

Using the two fingers that were rubbing her clit, she inserts them, pumping them in and out before removing them and raising her hand back. I lean forward and suck on her glistening fingers, savoring the sweet taste of her cunt.

As good as her mouth feels and as sexy as she looks letting me possess her this way, I want her wrapped around me. I remove my cock and she takes a gasping breath of air, her face dripping from the moisture pooled from her mouth.

Using the corner of the sheet, I clean up around her lips. Hillary doesn't let anyone see her messy and undone, not even Marisa, but she lets me, and what a fucking privilege it is. I love dirtying up my proper girl.

Her lips are swollen, with the remnants of pink lacquer lingering in the corners, eyes glassy from her choking tears.

"You look so beautiful like this," I tell her as I settle my body over hers.

"Too many clothes." She starts pulling on my shirt, so I help her along, then begin unwrapping her from her cotton sundress. It's got ties on the shoulders and all along the back, making me feel like I'm unwrapping a present on Christmas morning.

Once I have her free, I take a moment to admire her as I'm straddled over her, preventing her from being able to move.

The wine has loosened her up enough to be slightly more

uninhibited than she normally would be and she starts toying with her breasts, teasing me.

"Did I give you permission to touch yourself?"

Her tongue darts out, dampening her lips, and she shakes her head slowly, eyes full of fire.

"Sorry, daddy." Her voice is all sweet honey, dripping in false innocence.

I capture her lips with mine and fill her in one thrust. She sighs into my mouth and palms my behind, pushing me forward until I can't go any further.

I thrust in and out of her in a way I haven't since we had Josephine. At first, I was gentle with her, worried I would hurt her, which eventually turned into quick romps when the opportunity arose because Josephine is still in our bedroom. But now that it's just us two, no baby monitor, no rush, no one but us, I fuck her rough, yet deliciously slow. I take my time, fucking her in a rhythm that has her tits bouncing and her head tossed back, the sweetest noises escaping from her. My mouth sucks on her neck as my hands wander, pinching her nipples and circling her clit, digging into her newly rounded hips that I can't seem to get enough of. I want it to last forever, but soon I'm coming, and she's right there with me. Her pussy clenches around my cock and I hold her body against mine as she rides the wave of her orgasm.

We stay tangled in each other, our chests both heaving. Her hair is matted around her forehead, slick with sweat and a satisfied glow that already has me growing hard again.

"That was..." she moans, her words dying.

"I know," I tell her, taking a breath.

"Definitely not saying no to another weekend away, in case you were wondering."

I chuckle, tugging her closer and giving her forehead a kiss. "Good. Because we have a lot of time to make up for." I angle my hips so she can feel my hard cock against her thigh.

"How are you already ready again?" Her voice is mock-appalled but her hips are already twisting, trying to rub up against me.

"You see, I have this incredibly sexy wife. One who I can't seem to get enough of."

A smile takes over her face, warmth blooming beneath her skin. "Is that so?"

I give her a kiss meant to be soft, but quickly turns hungry and desperate. "Absolutely."

CHAPTER 10

Archie

TOUGHER THAN SHE LOOKS

THEN

I take the stairs slowly, my hand dragging along the banister as I go. Emma's voice is a low murmur through the cracked door at the end of the hall, mingling with Hillary's hushed tone. I don't want to interrupt, but I need to at least make sure everything's settled before I give them space. That's what I tell myself, anyway.

When I get to the top, the door creaks, and they both look up. Emma gives me a pointed look, one that says, *Give her a break, don't make it weird*, so I force a half-smile, hoping it looks easygoing. I nod at Hillary, trying to seem...I don't know, brotherly, maybe? But that doesn't really work, especially not when my eyes snag on the way her curly hair falls around her shoulders, a bit messy from the night's events, but still so pretty. My fingers rub together, imagining what it might feel like between them. I shouldn't be thinking that. I shouldn't be thinking a lot of things currently on my mind. She's here because she's been through enough for one night, and my job is to help. Not to do whatever this is.

Clearing my throat, I shift my weight and glance around the room. "You alright? Need anything?"

She shakes her head, offering a small smile, polite but tired. "No, I think I'm all set. Thank you for letting me stay."

"Of course," I say, maybe a little too quickly, and I feel Emma's gaze sharp on me. I turn to go, but can't quite bring myself to leave just yet. "If you need anything—water, an extra blanket, whatever—I'll be downstairs for a bit. Or Emma can help you with all that."

She nods, attempting to look brighter, and I can tell she's trying to put me at ease, which just makes me feel even more ridiculous. This isn't about me. It's about making her feel comfortable here. I turn and finally head back downstairs, ignoring the fact that my thoughts continue to wander back to her.

As I'm checking the locks, I fight the urge to run up and check on her again. *What is wrong with me?*

There's a knot in my chest I can't quite loosen, and it's not just concern. It's her. The way she looked back at me, polite and grateful, like I'd done her this massive favor, when I've done nothing.

Shaking my head, I keep moving. Back behind the bar, I distract myself with tidying, wiping down the bar top, even though it doesn't need it because Will took care of it. After the commotion, Will shut down, as it was closing time anyway. He headed off as soon as the last patron left.

Emma joins me a few minutes later, eyeing me carefully, like she's waiting for me to admit something. I don't plan on giving her the satisfaction.

"Thanks for letting her stay," she says eventually, crossing her arms as she leans against the counter. "I know you sort of offered, but I should've ran it by you first, in case you were only trying to be polite."

"I wouldn't have told her to stay if I didn't mean it," I tell her, and it's true. Emma is like Will, she likes to take in strays. Me? Not so much. Hillary is the exception. I *want* her here, even though we hardly know each other. It doesn't make any sense. If Emma hadn't already insisted she stay, I would have. I'm not sure what to make of that.

Emma raises an eyebrow, catching on faster than I'd like. "You okay?"

"Yes, why wouldn't I be?" I keep my tone casual, but she doesn't buy it.

"Because you look as if you're ready to climb the tower like a knight in shining armor." Her cheeky smile only further annoys me.

"Isn't it past your bedtime?"

She sticks her tongue out at me and turns her back, picking up the remaining glasses on a table that didn't get cleared.

We're quiet for a stretch as the low hums of a sappy Ed Sheeran song flow through the speakers.

"It's okay to care enough about her to want to help. She's had quite the night," Emma says, all hints of her humor from earlier gone.

I nod, trying to not focus on the flicker of longing that sneaks in with the worry. "I just...I don't know. It's been a weird night, and seeing someone like her treated like that. It doesn't sit well, you know? I had to do something. This seems like the bare minimum."

Emma's expression eases, some of the hardness slipping away as she glances toward the stairs, her gaze going distant. "She's tougher than she looks. I bet she could've handed him his balls if she'd been alone. But you were there." She looks back at me. "That's got to count for something cosmic at the very least. Right place, right time." Her jaw tightens. "That shithead's lucky it wasn't me he tried dragging out the door.

Otherwise, you'd be helping me mop up the blood from what was left of him."

"Ah, yes Em. We all know you're ruthless." I laugh, shaking my head. Emma is all talk, but as the little one of us three, we let her think she's both bark and bite.

Emma leaves to go to sleep, and I focus back on cleaning, trying to scrub the thoughts out of my head. Thoughts I shouldn't be having. Thoughts that make me feel like an idiot, like I'm crossing some invisible moral line.

But as much as I tell myself to ignore it, I know that when I lie down tonight, I'll be wondering if she's asleep, if she's okay. And I'll want her to stay...maybe longer than just tonight.

Now

Flat Stone, the restaurant inside Ledger Winery, feels cozy and lively this morning. Marisa's holding court at the center of the table, grinning ear to ear. Her shitty ex never let her be the center of attention, but not Ethan. The man hates social situations like they're a plague, a testament to how much he cares about her to suffer through this just to make her happy.

The long table is packed with all of Ethan's siblings, his parents, and Marisa's dad and his wife and step children. Even some of Marisa's coworkers are in attendance.

I give Ethan an approving nod and he stiffly returns it before giving Marisa all of his focus.

"A French omelet for the lady," a heavily tattooed man says to Marisa as he sets down her plate. He's clearly the chef, and if I'm not mistaken, Ethan's younger brother as well.

"Thanks, Shane," Marisa says, confirming my suspicions.

Shane clears his throat to get everyone's attention. "Now

everyone listen up. This is my trial run to prove I can handle the breakfast shift. Next to your flatware you'll find a card to leave a rating and review of your meal. Please be honest and let everyone know how amazing it was because I'm a great fucking chef."

"Humble, too," Archie whispers in my ear and I laugh quietly.

"Language young man," Ethan's mom yells out.

Shane snickers and heads back to the kitchen while servers bring everyone their meals.

I ordered a breakfast scramble and I hate to admit it but it's the best one I've ever had. He's cocky, but he's not wrong; he really is a great chef.

"Bloody hell," Archie says between bites of his steak and eggs. "Fucking delicious."

"I know," I tell him. "Guess we'll be leaving a five-star review."

"Guess so," Archie murmurs, taking another bite and glancing over at Shane, who's now lurking near the kitchen door with his arms crossed, watching our reactions with a smug smile. "Can't say he doesn't deserve it, though. Kid knows his way around a pan."

I take a sip of my coffee, savoring the rich, smooth taste. Archie has managed to convert me into a tea drinker, but I still prefer coffee. "I wouldn't mind coming back here again. We'll have to come visit soon. And maybe we can plan a trip somewhere else in the meantime. Just us again."

Archie smiles. "I like the sound of that. I think if we came here again without Josephine, Marisa would blow her lid."

"You're probably right." Marisa already has baby fever and Ethan hasn't even proposed yet.

Across the table, Marisa is laughing at something Ethan has whispered in her ear, and I can't help but notice how at ease they both look—like they've finally settled into each other's lives without any reservations. Ethan has his arm draped over the back of her chair, fingers grazing her shoulder, and she leans into him naturally, like it's the most comfortable place in the world.

As brunch continues, I get lost in the energy around the table. The clinking of glasses, bursts of laughter, and a drone of conversations weave around us. I catch snippets of Ethan and his dad talking about the winery plans for next year, Elyse whispering something mischievous to her sisters, and Archie sharing a story about our weekend with Ethan's parents, who listen with rapt attention.

By the time the plates are cleared, and Shane comes around to collect his feedback cards, Marisa's eyes are shining with gratitude. "Thank you, everyone. This is more than I could've asked for. I feel incredibly lucky."

Ethan leans over and presses a kiss to her cheek, earning a chorus of "awws" from around the table. She laughs, hiding her face, and murmurs, "Okay, okay. Enough mushy stuff."

It fills my heart to see her surrounded by people who truly care about her, people who encourage her to take up space and just be herself—it's exactly what she deserves.

Eventually, everyone starts standing to say their goodbyes, exchanging hugs and promises to meet up again soon. Marisa wraps me in a tight hug, lingering for an extra second.

"Thank you for coming," she says softly, her voice thick with emotion. "It means so much to me. I know it was hard to leave Josephine even though you tried to pretend it wasn't. Thank you."

I squeeze her back. "I wouldn't have missed it for anything. Happy birthday, sweetie." As she pulls away, I reach in my purse to retrieve a small gift box. I hand it to her and she reluctantly takes it, looking suspiciously amused.

"I told you not to get me anything."

I shrug. "I know. I didn't listen."

Tearing it open, she pulls out the first part of the gift. A locket necklace with a picture of her and Josephine on the day she was born.

"Oh, I love this picture," she says, smiling as she stares at it.

"Turn it around." I bite my lip, waiting to see her reaction once she reads the engraving.

It takes her a moment and then her gaze meets mine, her brown eyes slightly misty. "Are you sure? But what about Emma? Won't she be upset?"

I shake my head. "I asked her too. Josephine could use two badass godmothers."

She places her hands over her chest, clutching the necklace against her. "I'm so honored."

Before this turns into a sappy mess, I force her to open up the rest of the gift. "Look, I know gift cards are lame, but I know you, and you would never spend that much money on yourself at a spa, so I'm doing it for you."

"Hillary! This is way too much," she says while eyeing the amount on the gift card.

"They were having a gift card sale," I lie, and she knows it.

"If it makes you feel that uncomfortable, I suppose I could join you." I waggle my brows, and she takes the bait.

"A spa day? Just us two? I won't say no to that."

We hug again and as we pull apart, she whispers, "Have a safe trip back and text me the second you get home, or I'll worry."

Marisa tosses me one last smile before she turns to the rest of the group. As Archie and I make our way toward the exit, I glance over my shoulder, watching Marisa laugh with Ethan and his family.

Outside, Archie pulls me close, slipping an arm around

my shoulders as we head to the car. "Well, the holiday's finished now, love," he says, his breath warm against my ear. "Back to reality."

As we drive away, I get settled into my seat. Only four hours until I get to hold my baby girl, and I can't wait.

CHAPTER 12

Hillary

PROPER ENGLISH TEA

THEN

"No, everything is fine. Kyle and I are planning to do some sightseeing today. Busy day," I say with a laugh, but it feels so disingenuous I'm sure my mom can tell I'm hiding something.

She pauses but doesn't question me. "Okay, then. Be safe. Love you."

"Love you," I say, holding back tears. If she knew everything, she'd have my dad ready to kill Kyle and probably send an army to come get me.

I set my phone down and wrap the blanket tighter around my shoulders. I can't believe I actually stayed here, with strangers, and yet it was the best night of sleep I've gotten in a long time. Weird.

Emma already left for class, leaving me alone with Archie, but he has yet to emerge from his bedroom. She reassured me he's as harmless as a kitten and wouldn't do anything to make me uncomfortable while she's gone. It wasn't necessary, but I appreciated her concern.

I hear his footsteps and tense, preparing myself for the wave of awkwardness. Not to say that I've never gone home with a bartender before, but this whole damsel-in-distress situation is a first for me. Part of me feels like a one-night stand would be less bizarre than this.

"Mornin'," he says as he walks into the living room dressed in a suit with his hair slicked back, face freshly shaven.

Holy hell.

I dip my chin and avert my eyes. He looked good last night, but now he looks really, really good. A blush skirts across my cheeks, heating me from the inside out.

"Morning," I reply, way too high-pitched to sound normal.

If I had known he was going to walk in here dressed like that, I might have made more of an effort in my appearance. Emma is much taller than me, and her clothes hang off my arms and legs, making me look like a rag doll. The rat's nest of hair piled on my head doesn't help matters.

"Did I just hear you tell someone you're going to be sight-seeing with Kyle today?" Archie asks, his eyes narrowed in suspicion.

"My mom," I explain. "She's a worrier, and it's better if I tell her everything in person instead of over the phone."

He nods slowly, but doesn't press me.

"Do you happen to know the best way to get to the embassy? I'm going to need an emergency passport to get back home."

I hadn't thought of it until I read through the hundreds of threatening texts from Kyle trying to get me to meet up with him in exchange for my things and passport. As if holding them hostage is going to persuade me into seeing him again. Everything is replaceable, especially shitty men.

"I actually only work until noon on Fridays. I can take you, if you'd like? Navigating this city can be a bit daunting."

He pauses, studying me, and it's as if his gaze is penetrating past the easy demeanor I'm trying to portray. "Besides, Em only has one class today and I'm sure she'll want to talk your ear off. Poor girl doesn't get out enough." He laughs. "You might want an escape."

I think that's why I felt okay with staying here last night. Emma immediately made me feel like I was a friend, and I could really use a friend right now. Archie doesn't give me those same feelings. In fact, he makes me feel things that are pretty inconvenient given I just had an altercation with my now ex-boyfriend. Not to mention there will be forty-eight hundred miles between us when I fly home.

"Noon sounds great." I fidget with my thumbs, feeling awkward yet stupidly nosy at the same time. The nosiness wins. "So, what kind of engineer are you?"

He looks caught off guard by my question, maybe surprised I remembered him telling me he wasn't actually a bartender.

"Aeronautical," he says hesitantly. "I've always liked planes."

I think all engineers are fairly smart, but I'm certain that's one of the more difficult kinds. He's probably incredibly intelligent, likely only adding to how stupid he must think I am. Just a silly American girl with bad taste in men.

Unable to find words that sound even mildly clever, I say the first thing that comes to mind. "That's cool. Planes are cool."

He breathes a smile. "Very cool." His mouth opens and closes a few times before he continues, and somehow I become more at ease seeing that he's also unsure of how to act. "And you? Do you have a job back home? Wherever home is."

"Real estate. In Seattle. My parents have a commercial real estate firm, so I went to work for them after college. It's kind of a family business."

"So, you're close, then? With your family."

"Incredibly. My mom is my best friend, I tell her everything—" I break off, my face pinching at my current predicament. "Well, almost everything."

His lips tighten into a polite smile, and my breath drags out. I'm unsure of what to do or say next. I shift in my seat and some of the hair falls loose from my haphazard topknot, a long tendril sweeping across my vision. Swiping it away, my thumb brushes across my cheekbone, and I wince at the contact. I didn't think Kyle had slapped me that hard, not hard enough to actually leave a mark. I stand and rush over to the mirror near the door, Archie watching me curiously. My cheek is red, not bruised, thankfully. At least there's that. It looks more like a sunburn, not something noticeable.

As I stare at my reflection, it's like it didn't happen to me, it happened to someone else. I'm not the kind of woman who gets hit. That happens to other people, not me. Never me. How did this happen? When did I become such a poor judge of character?

"Here," Archie whispers.

My head whips away from my reflection and cranes to look up at him. Gently, he places a bag of frozen vegetables wrapped in a kitchen towel against my cheek. I think I'd cry if I wasn't so shocked.

"Thank you." My voice is a croak.

Our gazes meet, and the corner of his lips quirk up. "I wish I had steak on hand. A bag of peas will have to do."

My lips roll, biting a smile. I appreciate him trying to keep the situation light. The last thing I need right now is to crumble. I'm like a toddler that's just banged my head on a table—if no one says anything I won't cry, but the moment it's recognized, I'll fall apart.

"A bachelor without steak on hand? Unheard of," I tease.

I hope my very poor attempt at finding out if he's single doesn't sound as obvious out loud as it felt coming out.

"I'll be sure to out myself the next time I meet up with my bachelor support group." His quick retort catches me off guard, causing my pulse to jump under the knowing smirk he's shooting my way.

We stare at each other like we both want to say more but don't. Silently, he wraps his hand around my wrist and brings it up to meet his other one, the one holding frozen vegetables against my cheek. Our hands brush as he situates mine to replace his, our gazes never wavering. My fingers curl around the plastic bag, making a crunching noise as I grip the cold peas. If the circumstances were different, I might lean forward and kiss him. Instead, I take a step back, shaking my head of silly thoughts, like kissing a man I barely know.

We continue staring at each other for a suspended second before he eventually nods, satisfied I can hold the bag myself, and then starts working around the kitchen. I stay rooted in place, more frozen than the vegetables.

"There's tea if you'd like some. The kettle is still warm. If you'd prefer a coffee, there's a café downstairs and around the corner."

His conversation shift breaks me out of my trance. "Tea is fine." I walk toward the kitchen, not wanting him to feel like he has to cater to me by making me tea when I'm sure he's trying to get out the door to go to work.

I grab a mug off the shelf and choose a breakfast tea, setting the tea bag in the mug before pouring the hot water from the kettle over it.

I feel Archie's eyes on me but pretend I don't.

"Do you want milk and sugar?"

I still and then look at him. He smiles at my confusion.

"Milk and sugar? For tea?"

He laughs, and the sound is so warm it makes my stomach

flutter. "Yes, some people like milk and sugar in their tea. Have you not had a proper tea since you've been here?"

I shrug, unable to contain my smile at his perplexed expression. "We'd only just arrived the day before last. So, no, I haven't had proper English tea."

He laughs again, shaking his head at me. Walking back from the fridge, he sets a pint of milk and a box of sugar cubes next to my mug. "Since I'm assuming you're usually a coffee drinker, you'll probably like a splash of milk and sugar in your tea. Plus, the tea you chose is quite bitter and harsh, might need the edge taken off."

He's standing close, close enough for me to catch a whiff of his aftershave, and it's intoxicating, returning those ridiculous thoughts, like leaning into him would be a good idea.

I add milk and two sugar cubes to the tea. "Okay, I guess I'll take your word for it."

Our eyes meet, and I think I'm imagining it, but he's not looking at me like I'm an inconvenient houseguest. He's not looking at me like a victim who needed rescuing. He's looking at me like he spotted me from across the room and hasn't been able to tear his eyes away since.

His blue eyes look almost gray. Like a comforting gray sky stretching wide and steady overhead.

A horn blares outside, breaking the spell.

Archie clears his throat. "Well, I'll be off then. See you at noon."

"See you," I reply. Once the door is closed, I set my mug down and bury my face in my hands while I slump against the counter. What the hell was that?

CHAPTER 13

Archie

GREAT LITTLE CITY

THEN

At the office, the familiar thrum of chatter and the soft clicking of keyboards greets me like déjà vu. Same place, same people, different day.

"Morning, Archie!" Hugo, my office mate, calls out as he walks by, balancing a stack of drawings in one hand.

I wave back, settling into my desk and booting up my computer. I glance at my emails—mostly mundane updates, a couple of project requests. Just another day at the work, which is good, because I'm finding myself incredibly distracted by the curly-headed blonde beauty back at my flat.

As I'm scrolling through my inbox, my boss Jasper, strides in, his tie slightly askew and a look of determination on his face. That's never a good sign. He heads straight for me, and I sit up a little straighter.

"Hemingway," he says, his tone serious. "Do you have a minute?"

"Yes, of course," I say, trying to sound casual, but my gut twists a bit. It's never good when he uses my surname.

"As you know, we're expanding the fleet." He glances around the office before leaning closer. "I'm sure you heard I'm sending a team to represent us at a meeting at Boeing headquarters next week. Edward was supposed to be lead, but he called this morning and dropped out due to a family emergency. Interested in taking his spot? I know it's last minute, but you're the only one qualified to take his place."

The words hit me like a jolt. I was prepared for something bad, not considering he had something good to say. "Absolutely," I reply without hesitation. This is a big deal—an opportunity to help shape the direction of the airline and potentially score some influence with management.

The fact that Boeing is also in Seattle and Hillary lives in Seattle has absolutely nothing to do with my excitement. Nothing at all.

Oh, who am I kidding? It has everything to do with Hillary.

"Great," he says, nodding. "It'll be a trip full of meetings, and I want you to prep some questions about the new models we're considering. They've got some exciting developments, and we need to know how they'll fit into our plans."

"Got it." My mind is already racing. "When do you want to meet to go over everything? And how long will this trip be?"

He gives me a quick rundown of the schedule, but I barely hear him, too overwhelmed.

"We'll have you and the rest of the team stay the entire week. You'll fly out Monday. You ever been to Seattle?"

I shake my head wordlessly, not wanting a tremble in my voice to give me away.

"Great little city, and you'll feel right at home with the weather. Get in some sightseeing while you're there."

My mind is buzzing with excitement, more so for the chance to possibly see Hillary again rather than the career opportunity that it is. I'm likely getting ahead of myself, seeing as she doesn't even have a passport to get back home yet. It would be something, though, to get to see her again, with a legitimate excuse. Maybe I'll bring it up later after we go to the embassy. The last thing I want is to come off like some creepy guy.

After he walks away, I can't help but grin to myself. I'm deep in thought when Hugo peeks over the partition.

"What's got you looking so pleased?"

"I just got assigned to replace Edward for the Boeing meeting next week," I say, because I'm not about to tell him I'm more excited over a woman than anything job related. "They're expanding the fleet, and I'll be heading up the team."

"Wow, that's amazing!" he exclaims, his eyes wide with excitement. "You deserve it, Archie. You've been putting in the work."

"Thanks," I reply, feeling slightly guilty that I'm not more appreciative of what this could do to boost my position within the company. That should be the only thing I'm focused on. "I just hope I don't screw it up."

"You won't," he reassures me before turning back to his desk.

With Hillary weighing heavily on my mind, I dive into my prep work, trying to focus on my actual job. But in the back of my thoughts, she's still there, taking up space. It's more than her beauty, it's like an unspoken connection. Maybe I'm the only one feeling it, but on the off chance that I'm not, I can't help but see it as a sign from the universe that I'll be heading to Seattle next week—coincidently, the very city my unlikely houseguest is from. It has to be a sign. I feel foolish for even thinking such a thing, evidence that Emma has been talking her manifestation and astrology facts to me too much lately. I should be focusing on my job. This is my career, my future, and I can't let anything distract me from that, right?

I swing the front door open, half-expecting to find Hillary still standing in the kitchen exactly where I left her. Instead, I walk in to find her pacing near the window, looking more put together than this morning. She's wearing her clothes from last night, a dress made of sweater-like material paired with a raincoat and rain boots. Her wild, curly hair flows freely around her shoulders. She looks beautiful.

I set my keys on the table in a loud clank, in case she didn't hear me walk in. "Ready to head out?"

She turns, her expression looking relieved, like she's excited to see me. More like she's excited to get a passport and get out of here. I shouldn't let my thoughts create false realities.

"Ready as ever." She grabs her bag and giving me a quick, almost shy smile.

"Did Emma not come by after class?" I hold the door open for Hillary to walk through. One of her stray curls drags across my chest as she passes, and like a dog on a leash, it pulls me to follow right behind her. She walks ahead of me as I try to not stare at the way her dress hugs her ample bottom.

"She did, you just missed her. She left to meet up with a study group."

I nod silently, completely uninterested in Emma, I simply prefer to keep Hillary talking to continue listening to her melodic voice.

As we step outside, I glance at her, making sure she's actually up for this. Navigating the embassy can be a nightmare on a good day, let alone after everything she's been through. "You sure you want to do this today?"

She nods, taking a deep breath as we start down the street toward my car. "I am. I just want this over with."

I can understand that. And as much as I hate that she's

tangled up in such a mess, there's a part of me that's glad I can help her, even if it's just getting her to a government building.

The U.S. Embassy is located in the Nine Elms district, surrounded by crowded tourist attractions and heavy city traffic. The drive takes a little under an hour. It probably would've been shorter to take the tube, but I didn't feel like spending what little time I have left with Hillary on public transport. Plus, I would've missed out on her horrible singing voice as she sang along to the Top 100 radio station I had playing. It might've been the best drive I've ever been on.

We luck out with parking, but it's still a trek getting to the front of the building.

"So, what happens after you get the passport sorted?" I ask as we dodge around a few tourists clustered around a street performer.

She shrugs, her face clouding over. "I'm not sure. Probably head home, figure out what's next. I didn't quite think everything through, so unfortunately all but one of my credit cards are with Kyle. I think I have enough to get home, but if I don't, I might have to tell my parents what happened, and I'm not looking forward to that." Her voice is tight, like she's trying to appear calm when I highly doubt she feels anything close to it. I'm glad I punched him, but now I wish I had punched him at least twice.

Subconsciously, I flex my hand, and Hillary notices.

"How's your hand? I hope you didn't hurt yourself."

The worry in her eyes makes my chest tighten with an ache I'm not sure I'm capable of ignoring. "All good. Nothing a frozen bag of peas can't fix."

She giggles, and it's fucking adorable. "That's good."

We walk in silence for a bit after that, neither of us pushing it. When we finally reach the embassy, she looks at the entrance with an expression that's a mix of dread and determination.

I stop, reaching out to put a hand on her shoulder without thinking about it. "Just tell them the truth," I say, giving her shoulder a gentle squeeze. "I'm sure it won't be a problem getting a new passport. If you need anything, I'll be right out here."

She glances up at me, her expression softening just a bit, and gives a small nod. "Thanks, Archie. For...everything. Really."

I nod back, not trusting myself to say much else. As she heads inside, I lean against the rail outside, watching her until she disappears through the door. Part of me knows my little crush is quickly becoming not so little. Leave it to me to start liking a woman I have no business liking. One who lives a whole ocean away. I should just walk away now, cut all ties. It would be for the best. But another part of me knows I'm not going anywhere. It's been less than twenty-four hours, and this woman already has me wrapped around her finger. And the worst part? She doesn't even know it.

CHAPTER 14

Archie

I'D MOVE HERE IN A HEARTBEAT

Now

As we drive down the winding road away from Red Mountain, I can't help but glance over at Hillary. She's leaning back in her seat, sunglasses on, a relaxed smile playing on her lips. The weekend was exactly what we needed—a break from everything. Just the two of us.

I reach over, slipping my hand into hers. "I'm really glad we did this. I was worried you would back out, and I'm really, really happy you didn't."

She turns to me, squeezing my hand. "No work, no baby, no distractions. It was perfect." She sighs.

I chuckle, nodding. "True. And it's not every day Mum's able to take on babysitting duty for a whole weekend. She might need a holiday herself from looking after Josephine."

Hillary laughs, and the sound fills the car with warmth. "She probably does, even though I'm sure she loved it. Compared to the chaos she gets from Will and Sarah's boys, Josephine is like a walk in the park."

We fall into a comfortable silence, the hum of the car and

the views rolling by keeping us company. I don't say it, but leaving almost feels bittersweet. I'm eager to see our daughter, I just hope it doesn't mean watching Hillary slowly slip away again.

"I was thinking about when I came to Seattle for the first time. Do you remember it?"

"Of course I do." She laughs, a bit sheepish. "Like I could ever forget. I remember thinking I was losing my mind because I already liked you so much and we hardly knew each other."

"I would say we got to know each other quite well during that visit. A few times, actuallly." I wink at her.

She smirks, face flushing. "You could say that."

"You know," I say after a moment. "It was the first time I realized I was falling in love with you. I was probably in love with you the second I handed you that glass of whiskey, but I knew for sure something unlike anything I'd ever experienced was happening between us. I knew you were going to change my whole life."

She lifts her sunglasses, letting them push back her hair, and her brows raise in surprise. "Really? That early on? I know I was falling fast, I didn't realize it was happening just as fast for you."

"How could I not be?" I keep my eyes on the road as my face floods with heat. "I didn't want to scare you off. When I got back, I started looking into citizenship and how I could make my job work in Seattle."

Hillary's quiet for a beat, and when I glance over, she's smiling softly at me. "I didn't know you started doing all that so soon after."

"It just hit me, all at once. I'd never planned to live anywhere but home. But there I was, standing in the middle of the street on our way to dinner, watching you walk ahead of me like you owned the whole city, and I thought, 'Yeah, I'd move here in a heartbeat if it meant I could be with her.'"

Her tear-filled eyes meet mine and she squeezes my hand. "Well, I'm glad you did."

"So am I," I say, my voice a little husky. "It was worth every bit of change. I wouldn't trade any of it."

We fall silent, but it's the good kind of silence. The kind where you don't need words to fill the space because everything important has already been said.

After a while, she settles back in her seat, and I keep my focus on the road, feeling more grounded than I've felt in a long time. It's funny how a weekend away can remind you of all the reasons you made the choices you did, of everything you've built together.

And as we head back toward home, I know this—this life we've created—is exactly where I was meant to be.

CHAPTER 15

Hillary

SO, FUNNY THING

THEN

The embassy waiting room is cold, sterile, and as far from home as I could possibly feel. But I got exactly what I came here for, my passport approval in hand. Relief washes over me—I'm officially free to leave London and get back to my life, my job, my apartment, everything I put on hold because of Kyle's ridiculous stunts. But there's something else tugging at the edges of my thoughts, something I don't want to admit.

I'll miss Archie. I feel silly even thinking the thought. I barely know the man. But the more time we spend together, the more I want to know. I want to know everything.

I can't help it, and just thinking of him has me blushing. It's laughable, really—he's just been so kind, helping me navigate this entire nightmare without making me feel like a complete burden. But there's something about the way he's always looking out for me, the way he's managed to make me feel safe and steady, that's harder to let go of than I'd thought.

He's waiting for me in the lobby, his warm smile greeting me as I walk the long hallway toward him.

"I take it everything went smoothly?"

I lift the paperwork in my right hand. "All squared away. They said it would normally take a few days, but after I explained the situation, they were able to expedite things."

"That's good, you'll be home before you know it." He smiles, but it doesn't reach his eyes.

I return the same fake smile.

"Well..." I drag. "If you ever find yourself in the states, specifically the Pacific Northwest portion of the country, I owe you a drink. Several drinks..."

He clears his throat, looking a bit bashful. Shifting his weight, he scratches the back of his neck like he's nervous. It's incredibly endearing.

"So, funny thing," he says, eyes darting to the floor. "I wasn't sure whether or not to mention this, because, well, it might sound a bit weird."

"Weird?" I echo, brows raised, more curious than ever.

He rubs his neck, his cheeks turning a little pink. "Yeah, uh, my job is actually sending me to Seattle next week. There's a project we're working on with Boeing, and they need someone to meet with their team."

My heart skips, and my whole face light up. "Really?"

"Yeah." He gives a short laugh, his gaze still not quite meeting mine. "I know it probably sounds creepy, especially since we've only just met. I didn't want you to think I was, you know, following you across the world."

I laugh, maybe a little too enthusiastically. "Archie, I definitely don't think that! That's—that's great news!"

He glances up at me, the surprise obvious on his face. "You think so?"

"Absolutely." Excitement bubbles within me, more than it

should, really. "I mean, you're basically a lifesaver at this point. I owe you so much more than a simple thank you. If you're free, I can show you around the city. Maybe even turn you into a coffee drinker." I giggle.

His eyes meet mine, filled with relief, along with something else, something that causes my stomach to swoop. "Well, in that case, maybe after you show me around, I can treat you to dinner?"

The way he says it, hesitant and just a little hopeful, makes my heart practically leap. I can barely contain my smile. "I'd like that. A lot, actually."

The air between us turns charged, and I realize I'm holding my breath. He came out of nowhere, and I don't think anything could've prepared me for him, but something inside me settles anyway. Like I've been bracing for impact my whole life and he's the first thing that doesn't feel like a collision.

"So how would you like to spend your last day in London?" Archie asks once we're settled in his car.

After my emergency passport was approved, I immediately booked the first flight home, a red-eye for tonight, so I have less than eight hours before I have to be at the airport.

My jaw drops slightly. "I'm fine to fend for myself, really. I don't want you to feel obligated to entertain me. Surely you have better things to do than touristy stuff in your own city."

His shoulders lift, and a corner of his lips quirk up. "It's no obligation. I *want* to show you around. And you'll get to return the favor in a few days."

He isn't being facetious or implying some underlying

innuendo, but my juvenile brain immediately starts imagining very inappropriate scenarios of us definitely returning favors to one another. The air has a cold bite to it, yet my skin is suddenly overheated, sweating even.

It takes me a moment to realize he's staring at me, waiting for my answer. In truth, I'd love nothing more than to spend my last hours in the city with him and I can't find it in myself to argue.

"Okay, if you want to play tour guide all day, then who am I to say no?"

He flashes me a devastatingly handsome smile, awakening a swarm of butterflies.

Oh, boy.

"Hillary, love, it would be my honor."

The car surges forward, stealing my breath before I can think too deeply that he just called me *love*. Maybe it's common to say around here, but common or not, it felt special when he directed it at me.

While his attention is focused on the traffic before us, I steal a glance at him. There's a pink flush on his cheeks and his jaw is set tight, like he wants to smile but is holding it back. My lips press, trying to reign in the girlish giggle wanting to burst out.

I think Archie likes me and I think I might like him right back.

He expertly maneuvers the heavy traffic, looking very determined for our next stop. I sit back, not asking questions, letting him fully control today's itinerary. I don't care where we go or what we do, I'm just happy to spend time with him.

Our first stop is Buckingham Palace, where the sheer grandeur of the place takes my breath away. The gilded gates and the vast expanse of the Queen's Garden make it feel like stepping into a royal fairytale. Tourists are scattered everywhere, cameras snapping, children waving at the guards in their stoic uniforms.

Archie leads me toward the front gates, his hand grazes mine briefly to guide me through the crowd. It's nothing, just a small, casual gesture, but it sends a jolt of electricity through me.

"Obligatory photo op," he says, pulling out his phone.

I smirk. "Oh, so now you're one of *those* tourists?"

He shrugs, an easy grin spreading across his face. "When in London…"

I roll my eyes but let him maneuver me into position. "Fine, but don't make me look awkward."

"I would never," he promises with mock seriousness, holding up his phone.

The first photo is fine, but then he does something I don't expect. "Say 'cheese'!" he teases in an exaggerated American accent.

I burst out laughing just as he snaps the next photo.

"Perfect," he declares, showing me the image.

My mouth is open mid-laugh, my cheeks rosy and wind-touched from the cold. I want to hate it, but I don't.

"It's terrible," I mutter, though a smile plays on my lips.

"It's perfect," he insists, his eyes soft. "You're laughing and that makes it perfect."

The way he says it makes me stop for a moment. I don't know if he means to sound so earnest, but my heart squeezes in my chest.

We move on, wandering past the palace and through St. James's Park. My boots crunch against the gravel pathway, the crisp air carrying the scent of fresh rain. Archie points out random trivia about the park, and I hang onto every word.

"You're oddly good at this," I say as we sit on a bench overlooking the lake.

"At what?"

"Being a tour guide. Should I be worried this is your go-to first date routine?"

He chuckles, the sound low and warm. "If this were a date, Hillary, trust me, you'd know."

My breath catches. His words float in the air between us, and for a long beat, I'm not sure how to respond.

"Well, you're doing a decent job," I say, hoping my tone sounds lighter than the fluttering in my chest.

"Just decent? Ouch."

I roll my eyes, nudging him with my elbow. "You've got a few hours left to win me over. Let's see where this next stop is, *shall we?*"

Archie smirks at my terrible attempt at a British accent, standing and offering me his hand. "Challenge accepted."

The next stop on Archie's list is Abbey Road. As soon as I realize where we are, I gasp.

"No way!"

"It would be criminal to skip past it," he says, smirking as he pulls the car into a spot along the street.

The iconic crosswalk is right in front of us, bustling with people recreating *that* photo. I scramble out of the car, practically vibrating with excitement.

"Are we seriously doing this?" I ask.

"You tell me," he replies, gesturing grandly toward the crosswalk.

Minutes later, I'm in the middle of the street, while a line of tourists wait to be next. Archie is setting up to take a picture of me, but I don't want to be alone in the picture. I want him in it with me.

I wave my hand, indicating he join me, and he shakes his head. "Oh, come on, don't make me do this alone!" I plead, making my best puppy dog face.

He groans but relents, jogging out to join me. Together,

we strike the classic pose, while a fellow tourist captures the image. On the last shot, whether it's exhaustion giving me the confidence or my own delusions, I reach my hand back, and he grabs it as our eyes connect. The flash goes off at the same moment.

"You guys are such a cute couple," our novice photographer says as she hands me back my phone.

I don't bother correcting her, and neither does Archie.

After Abbey Road, we hit a whirlwind of iconic spots.

Archie takes me to the Tower Bridge, where we walk along the river, and he points out landmarks I would've missed on my own. The sharp wind tugs at my coat as we stop for a moment to watch boats pass underneath.

"This is surreal," I say quietly, leaning on the railing.

"Good surreal or bad surreal?"

"Good," I reply, glancing at him. "Really, really good."

His lips curve, slow and entirely for me, and I let myself get lost in the warmth of his smile.

Next is a quick dinner from Borough Market, because my stomach growled embarrassingly loud. We share a flaky meat pie that's so delicious I moan without thinking. Archie freezes mid-bite, his ears turning red, and I pretend not to notice, though the memory will live rent-free in my mind forever.

Our last stop is Covent Garden. Twinkling lights hang overhead, and street performers draw small crowds in the square. We grab hot chocolates from a nearby stall, the cups warming our hands as we wander through the bustling atmosphere.

"You might want to rethink this whole engineering thing. I think you have a future in tour guiding."

Archie glances over, laughter tugging at his lips. "Your sightseeing standards must be very low."

"It's really more about the company for me," I reply before I can stop myself.

His gaze remains fixed on me for a stretch, and my cheeks flare under his attention.

As the sky darkens, he drives me to the airport. The car ride is quieter now, the day's adventures catching up with us. My chest tightens as we get closer to our destination, the looming reality of saying goodbye sinking in.

At the curb, Archie steps out and holds the door open for me. The buzz of the airport surrounds us, but all I can focus on is him.

"Well," I say, fiddling with the strap of my purse. "This has been the best day I've had in a long time."

"Me as well," he replies, shoving his hands into his coat pockets.

For a moment, neither of us moves. The air between us feeling thicker than the fog that's settled over the city.

"Safe flight, Hillary," he finally says, his voice rougher than usual.

I nod, swallowing the emotion building up in my throat. "Thank you. For everything."

Archie steps closer, and I hold my breath, wondering if this is it—if he's going to kiss me or just say goodbye. He does neither, so I close the distance, pulling him in for a hug. He stiffens and then wraps his long arms around me, tucking me against his chest. If I didn't have a flight to catch, I'd be tempted to never step out of this embrace. As we break apart, I reach up and cup either side of his face, pulling him down to my level, and give his left cheek a brief kiss.

He blushes, which makes me blush, too. Smiling at one another, our expressions say all the things we can't seem to voice.

"I'll see you in Seattle."

"Y-Yes," he stammers. "Seattle."

We share one last lingering stare before I turn and walk into the terminal, forcing myself not to look back.

It isn't until I'm seated at the gate, staring at the photo of us on Abbey Road, that I realize just how much I'm already missing him, even though I know I'll see him again in a few days.

Strangers yesterday, friends today. I'm not sure what the future holds, but something tells me Archie is in it.

CHAPTER 16

Archie

INCREDIBLY FORWARD

THEN

I've been in Seattle for almost a week, and it's been nothing but meetings and business dinners. Productive, yes, but utterly exhausting. I thought I would've had more of an opportunity to sneak away, but now it's my second to last day in the city, yet it's the first free moment I've had. All I can think of is how excited I am to see Hillary. Pathetic, really.

I stand outside Pike Place Market, shoving my hands deep into my coat pockets. The evening air carries the faint scent of saltwater from Elliot Bay, mingling with roasted coffee and fresh rain. A few street performers play nearby, the glow of the market's neon sign reflecting off the wet pavement.

And then I see her.

My heart stills, or quickens, I'm not quite sure. Likely both at once, setting off a chain reaction in my body.

Hillary's walking toward me, her cheeks bright pink from the cold, her scarf tucked snugly around her neck, curly hair flowing freely behind her. She's breathtaking.

"Archie," she greets, her voice warm, her smile even warmer.

"Hillary," I say, trying not to sound as nervous as I feel. "You look—" *Perfect. Stunning. Out of my league.* "Cold. Let's get inside."

She laughs, that sweet melodic sound that's been playing in my head on a loop since she left. "I'm fine, I'm wearing my wool coat. I usually avoid this area of the city because it gets so congested, but I figured I'd make an exception for you." She shoots me a wink, and I feel the tingle from it all the way down to my feet. "My plan is to do a quick pass through of the market and then grab dinner. I know you've been working all day and I would imagine you don't want to waste your evening standing in lines and fighting crowds."

Her face pinches like she's trying to contain a grimace, as if I'll protest in some way. She could've suggested diving with sharks in freezing water, and I'd still jump in right after her.

"Time spent with you is never a waste."

Her lips roll before a wide grin takes over. My answer seems to have pleased her because she simply nods and starts walking beside me.

As we begin strolling across the cobblestones to the entrance of the market, she loops her arm through mine, tucking herself closer to me.

Her touch sends a heated awareness through me that not even the chill in the air can penetrate. I glance down at her, a smile tugging at my lips. This close, I catch a whiff of the coconut smell coming off her curls. Seems fitting that she would smell tropical, when she radiates nothing but pure warmth.

Her eyes roam over my face, watching me with a glint. "This is going to sound silly, but I feel like we know each other."

My head falls back, a laugh escaping me. Her comment is

so unexpected, it takes me a beat to be able to respond. "Probably because we do. I punched your ex—" I pause, considering my next words. "He is an *ex*, right? Because if he's not, I might have to get Emma involved to talk some sense—"

"He's an ex," she breathes a laugh. "An ex with a restraining order and a police report filed."

I nod, relieved I don't need to ask her the prying questions I was holding back. "See, so I punched your ex, you stayed in my flat, and I showed you around one of the greatest cities in the world. I would say we know each other quite well."

Her mouth lifts in a delicate smile as our gazes lock. The moment extends, stretching past the tip-toe, past the politeness, past the caution. There's a spark, a *something*, buzzing in the air between us. Maybe not entirely named, but it's too undeniable not to notice.

She breaks away first, shaking her head with a quiet laugh. "Yeah, I guess you're right."

We continue walking, stopping in front of a flower vendor. She picks up a small bouquet and presses it to her nose, her eyes closing briefly as she inhales. "I love tulips. Usually they're sold out by this hour," She says under her breath, almost to herself.

"Then we're getting them." I pull out my wallet, already handing my card over to the vendor.

Her eyes widen as she protests. "You don't need to—"

"Too late, I already did."

She bites her lip, trying to hide a grin as she accepts the flowers. "Fine. But I'm getting you back for that."

"I'll risk it," I reply, and she laughs.

We move on through the market, pausing to admire displays and vendor stands. Many of the vendors are closed or in the process of closing. The further we go, the more the crowd thins.

"Sorry," Hillary says, when she catches me staring as a man

flips his sign from open to closed on the front of his booth. "I always forget this place turns into a dead zone after five."

Her mouth is downturned into the saddest little pout, only further drawing my attention to her rosy lips. I hate to see her disappointed, especially when spending time with her is enough for me.

"There is nothing to apologize for, honestly." My answer doesn't appear to satisfy her, so I grab her gently by the shoulders and turn her to face me. "I'm not here to walk through a market, I'm here to see you. Everything else is just filler."

My confession must surprise her because her eyes light up, a deep blush spreading across her face as a wisp of breath flows between her parted lips.

"I—uh—I...thank you."

My chest swells slightly as she unravels, her nerves mirroring the ones I'm struggling to keep beneath the surface.

"So," I say, drawing out the word. "Shall we head to dinner?"

My knowing smile meets hers, and her relieved exhale tells me there's at least an attraction. Still, she's probably not as far gone as I am.

"Yes!" she yells, before rearing back from her own outburst.

She spins on her heels and strides ahead, her steps full of determination. I stay rooted, admiring her. A streetlight near the market's exit shines a soft light, illuminating her hair like a golden halo. In this moment, she looks like an angel.

For a second, I forget to breathe. The world around us—the noise of the nearby traffic, the distant chatter of voices—fades into nothing. All I see is her, glowing like she belongs to some higher realm.

She pauses at the corner, glancing over her shoulder, sensing my gaze. Her eyes catch mine as amusement crosses her face. It jolts me out of my trance.

I force myself to move, closing the distance between us. "You always walk this fast, or are you trying to leave me behind?" I tease, my voice lighter than I feel.

Her lips twitch with the ghost of a smile. "Gotta keep up, Arch."

I like that she shortened my name, like we're familiar with each other.

I fall into step beside her, the night air cool against my skin. The halo effect is gone now, replaced by the glow of passing streetlights. But she doesn't need it. She still looks like something out of a dream. And I hope I never wake up.

"Two Seattle dogs, the works," Hillary tells the hotdog stand worker.

After the market, we took an Uber and ended up at a hotdog stand at the base of a grass-covered hill. When we arranged to get dinner, I assumed a restaurant. Not that I'm disappointed, more surprised than anything.

"What?" She laughs, catching me staring. "Too posh for a hotdog?" Her brows raise, she's teasing me.

I shake my head. "Never."

The worker hands her the two hotdogs wrapped in foil. She grabs them and pays faster than I can retrieve my card, apparently my payback for the tulips. Rather than put up a fight, I follow her up the path. Once we reach the top of the hill, she claims a nearby bench, patting it for me to join her. I set the tulip bouquet between us, and it's only when I get settled that I see the bench is situated to have a perfect view of the Seattle skyline.

"Here," she says as she hands me the foil wrapped hotdog, already working to unwrap hers. She waits for me to unwrap mine before bringing hers up to take a bite. "Alright," she says, holding it like it's some kind of trophy. "Moment of truth."

I lift an eyebrow but take a bite, the combination of flavors hitting me all at once. The cream cheese is unexpected but somehow perfect, balancing the heat of the jalapeños and the sweetness of the onions.

"Well?" she asks, watching me with curiosity.

I chew slowly, making a show of considering my response. "Okay," I finally admit. "Not bad. Different, though."

Her laughter rings out. "I'll accept that," she says, taking a bite of her own. A smear of cream cheese ends up on the corner of her mouth, and she doesn't seem to notice.

Without thinking, I reach over, brushing it away with my thumb. Her eyes flick to mine, the moment lingering longer than it probably should. My pulse quickens, and I have to remind myself to keep it together.

"You had a little something," I say, clearing my throat and leaning back.

She tilts her head, her smile easing at the edges.

"Thanks."

We eat in comfortable silence. She gazes at the view like she's seeing it for the first time, while I pretend to do the same. In truth, my attention is on her, watching from the corner of my eye, completely captivated.

When I stand to toss the foil wrapper, she also rises. We both freeze mid-motion, standing awkwardly close, and then burst into laughter.

"Guess we're synced up now." I step to the side to let her go first.

"Such a gentleman." She giggles, nudging me lightly with her shoulder as she passes. She tosses her wrapper into the bin with a triumphant grin. "Perfect aim."

I roll my eyes, taking my turn and mimicking her exaggerated toss. "Impressive, right?"

Totally," she says, her voice dripping with playful sarcasm.

We remain near the bench, the distant buzz of the city surrounding us. For a moment, neither of us speaks, and the air grows heavier. She looks up at me, her pouty lips aiming a warm smile at me, her eyes catching the light in a way that makes my chest tighten.

"So..." she starts, trailing off, her voice quieter now.

I step closer, my hands sliding into my pockets to keep from reaching for her too soon. "So," I echo, dipping my head. "What happens now?"

She doesn't answer right away, her attention shifting between my eyes and my mouth. The faintest smile tugs at her lips. "I don't know, Archie. You tell me," she whispers.

"Seeing as we're on borrowed time, may I be incredibly forward?"

She nods. "I think I would like that."

I move a step closer, just as she does the same. "I like you. And I know I'm just some random guy you met in a pub, but I haven't stopped thinking about you since you left and I think I would regret it for the rest of my life if I let this moment pass without kissing you."

Her breath catches, and for a second, she just looks at me, her lips parting as if she's about to say something. But instead of words, she closes the space between us, her hands sliding up to drag lightly against my chest.

"I like you too," she murmurs, her voice barely audible, and that's all I need.

I lean down, capturing her lips with mine. The world seems to tilt, everything else fading into the background. Her lips are soft and warm, and she kisses me back with a mixture of hesitation and boldness that makes my head spin. My hands find her waist, pulling her closer, and she melts into me like she's been wanting this just as much as I have.

The kiss deepens, slow and unhurried, yet electric. Our

bodies align in a way that's startlingly natural. As if we were always meant to fit here—like somewhere, somehow, I was shaped with her in mind.

When we finally pull apart, our foreheads rest together, both of us catching our breath.

"Wow," she whispers, her eyes fluttering open.

"Yeah," I manage, my voice rough and raspy. "Wow."

She takes a slight step back and, out of nowhere, starts laughing.

"What?" I ask, grinning despite myself.

She bites her lip, trying to stop, but it only makes her laugh harder. "It's just—if I'd known this was going to happen, I *definitely* wouldn't have suggested hotdogs for dinner."

I chuckle, brushing a thumb over her cheek. "Why not? I thought it was a charming choice."

Her laughter softens. "Sure, if you think cream cheese breath is a good prelude to kissing."

I lean in closer, my nose brushing hers. "Guess it didn't stop me."

Her smirk transforms into a smile, her voice dropping to a whisper. "Guess not."

And before either of us can overthink it, I kiss her again, laughing against her lips as she pulls me closer.

The following day I barely knock on Hillary's apartment door before it swings open. She's standing there in jeans and a soft sweater, her hair falling wildly around her shoulders. Just the sight of her hits me like a punch to the chest.

I can't help myself, and obliterate the space between us, cupping her face with my hands and kiss her.

She lets out a surprised sound, her hands gripping my coat as I press my lips to hers. For a split-second, I worry I've made a mistake, but then she kisses me back, her fingers curling into the fabric like she can't get close enough.

When we finally pull apart, both of us breathing hard, she looks up at me, her cheeks pink, lips swollen, eyes beautifully clear. "Hello to you, too," she laughs.

"Too much?" I ask, concerned I pushed her too far.

She shakes her head as she rises onto the balls of her feet, looping her arms around my neck and planting a featherlight kiss to my lips. "No, it was perfect."

My hand settles on the small of her back, keeping her close. Now that I've gotten to touch her, it seems to be all I want to do.

Saying goodbye to her yesterday evening was no easy feat. If I didn't have a morning packed with meetings, I'm not sure I would've left her at all. Thankfully, though, we wrapped up before lunch. Instead of going back to my hotel room with my team, I hightailed it straight to Hillary's. In a span of time that surprises even me, I've become completely captivated by this woman—caught in a spell I have no desire to escape.

Her arms are still wrapped around my neck as her lips brush against mine again, teasing, lingering. Any thought I had about coming on too strong vanishes. My fingers dig into the fabric of her sweater, her warmth seeping into me, her scent enveloping me.

When we break apart, her laughter is breathless. "So, what's the plan? I'm supposed to show you around, remember?"

I slide my hand up to her jaw, tilting her face so I can kiss her again. I never want to stop kissing her. "Right," I murmur against her lips. "What's first on the agenda?"

She hums, her voice muffled as my mouth moves to the curve of her neck.

"There's...there's the waterfront, and, oh—Gas Works Park," she says, the words morphing into a sharp inhale when I nip lightly at her skin.

"Mm-hmm," I murmur, barely paying attention. My fingers have found their way under the hem of her sweater, the softness of her skin stealing my focus entirely. "What else?"

Her laugh is quieter now, almost shy, as her hands tug at my coat, slipping it off my shoulders. "I thought about the Space Needle, but..." She pauses to pull me closer, her body pressing against mine. "We don't have to do everything."

"Good," I breathe, my jacket forgotten somewhere on the floor. "Because I'm not sure we're getting out of here."

She's leading me backward into the apartment now, her hands finding the buttons of my shirt. "You're probably right," she says, kissing me again, slower this time but no less intense. Her sweater joins my coat on the floor, and my palms skim the bare skin of her waist as my eyes drink her in. She shivers but doesn't pull away.

I stop for a moment, just enough to catch my breath. "Is this too fast?" I ask, my voice rougher than I mean it to be, but I have to know how she feels.

She looks up at me, her hands resting against my chest. "I don't know," she admits, a crease of worry etching across her forehead. "Is it for you?"

I shake my head, swiping her hair back from her face. "Not even a little. But I don't want to mess this up."

Her smile is gentle, her thumb tracing lazy circles over the fabric of my shirt.

"You're not messing anything up." She leans in, her lips pressing to mine again. "Unless you stop."

The last bit of hesitation melts away as I lift her into my arms, her laughter filling the space between kisses. Neither of us is in a rush, but neither of us can hold back any longer. By the time we reach her bedroom, I'm not sure which of us led the way, but it doesn't matter.

She pulls me down onto the bed, her hands threading through my hair.

"Archie?" she whispers, her voice quiet.

"Yeah?"

Her lips straighten as her brows pull together. "Am I just a story to you? The kind you tell people about—how you had a wild couple of days with some American girl, and then never spoke to her again. I'm not asking you for anything. I know we live in two different—"

I cut her off with a kiss, hoping it says all the things I haven't figured out how to put into words yet. When I pull back, I lean my forehead to hers, my hands cradling her face.

"Hillary," I say, my voice low. "You're not a story. And if you think I could walk away from you and never look back, then I've been making a terrible impression."

Her eyes search mine, a flicker of doubt still there. "We live in two different countries," she whispers, barely audible. "This doesn't exactly make sense."

I smooth my touch along her cheek, feeling the heat of her skin. "I know. But I also know you've been on my mind since the second I met you. And I don't want to lose whatever this is just because it doesn't fit into a neat little box."

Her lips part like she's about to respond, but instead, she pulls me back into a kiss, this one deeper, like she's filling with all the want she can't seem to express with words. Her hands find my shoulders, pulling me closer as if she's afraid to let go.

When we finally break apart, her breathing is uneven, her eyes locked on mine. "Okay," she murmurs, her voice steadier now.

"Okay." I smile, brushing a strand of hair from her face. "Because I'm just getting started."

I press my hips against hers, eliciting a high-pitched sigh.

Her hand comes around and palms my behind, forcing me to press into her harder. Through my pants, I can already feel how wet she is, how warm and inviting her pussy is for me. If I don't redirect things, I'll regret how quickly I blazed through this. She deserves to be taken care of, an attentive touch.

Sitting up, I remove my shirt. The moment it's off, her eyes flare.

"I like that you have red chest hair."

The sexiest blush skirts across her face, but her heated stare doesn't waver.

Taking advantage of her being momentarily distracted, I undo the button on her jeans and drag them down her beautiful legs. Her fingers slide under the band of her underwear as she lifts her hips and removes them.

She's confident, and I get the sense she's used to being in charge in these situations. Which only makes me that much more determined to give her everything no one else has, to let her lose herself.

Moving to lie on my stomach, I grab hold of her thighs and let myself inhale her sweet scent before going in for a taste.

Her breath is shaky as her hips roll.

"Oh, fuck," she moans as her fingers find my hair and tighten around the strands.

She begins to squirm, to start to pull away, but I keep her firmly in place.

"Archie, I need you inside me."

Fuck, do I want that. But I want her to orgasm at least once before we get that far.

I lift my mouth off her slightly. "You have to come on my tongue, love. Then I'll give you what you want."

Her thighs fall open wider, and I take it for the invitation it is and devour her pussy. Licking my way back up and down, rubbing her clit in measured circles, reading her cues and licking more, sucking harder. Soon, she's coming, and my tongue is flooded with her release. Before I've gotten a chance to fully enjoy her orgasm, she's pulling me up, dragging my face to hers, and capturing my mouth. Her hips grind against me, searching for the one thing that will fill her.

She twists to retrieve a condom from her nightstand, and together we slip it on. "I'm on birth control," she says under her breath.

I give her one last look, for confirmation that she still wants this as much as I do.

Wordlessly, her hand wraps around my cock, and she guides me to her entrance. She tilts up and our hips join, bringing me inside her achingly slow. Once I'm fully seated, I prop an elbow on either side of her head, my hands cradling her jaw as I kiss her and go deeper. Her thighs quake on either side of me as her body adjusts to me.

I hold us there, gazing down at her, in awe that this amazing woman has somehow become so much more than I could've ever imagined in such a short period of time.

Her eyes regard me as if she too understands. She nods her head, and I begin thrusting harder, increasing my pace. Our lips crash together, moving as feverishly against one another at the pace I'm rocking my hips. Her moans pass between us in a way that makes me feel more connected to her than I've ever felt.

"You feel incredible, love," I tell her as I bury my face in her neck, inhaling the coconut aroma.

"So do you," she breathes.

I feel her arm start to move, reaching between us, and I grasp her wrist just before she gets there. "I do the touching, let me make you feel good."

Her eyes widen, but before she can protest, my index finger is already circling her clit. Soon after, her pussy is clenching around my cock in pulses, and I know she's coming.

I follow right after, the waves of my orgasm ripple as I groan into her neck.

After a beat, I roll off her and gather her in my arms, a satisfied hum echoing between us.

"Fucking hell," I pant.

She lifts, propping up on an elbow, and stares at me with a smile I can only describe as completely spent and satisfied. "Fucking hell is correct." Her eyes sweep over me, blatantly checking me out.

"If you keep looking at me like that, we may never leave this bed."

She bites her lip, aiming her green eyes on my hardening cock. "Promise?"

We spend the rest of the day in bed, sightseeing forgotten. In between orgasms and snacks, I hold her, some part of me always needing to touch her. I'm not sure I'll ever get my fill of her, and I'm not sure I want to. Being with Hillary is unlike anything I've ever experienced.

When early morning comes, we're both quiet, neither of us wanting to acknowledge what comes next.

"You know, it's very inconvenient that you live on another continent," she says, slicing through the silence.

I stroke her shoulder with my knuckles as I hold her close. "I know, love. Believe me, I know."

She shifts, tucking her head so it's out of my sight. "If I never see you again, at least it was memorable. No regrets."

If I never see you again, it'll be the biggest regret of my life.

I press a kiss to the top of her head. "This isn't goodbye. We'll see each other again."

She lets out a hollow laugh, one that twists something inside me. "When? In a year? Two? Maybe we'll be like that movie and meet in the same spot once a year—until one of us dies."

The bluntness of her words stings, forcing me to confront

the reality of our situation. Suddenly, the urge to rethink every plan I've made about my life hits me like a gut punch. If there's anyone worth changing it all for, it's Hillary.

But I can't say that—not yet. She'd think I was certifiable. Instead, I try to steer the conversation toward something less daunting, more hopeful.

"I don't know if you realize this," I say, brushing her hair back, "but I work for an airline. Flying to see you—or you flying to me—isn't exactly impossible."

She hesitates, her gaze dropping as she fiddles with the sheets. "I guess…" she says softly, her voice laced with doubt.

I can't blame her for being unsure. We're still figuring each other out, and she has no reason to trust me yet. I lean down, trying to catch her stare.

"Have a little faith," I say, my voice gentler now.

She offers a wistful smile but still doesn't look at me, her fingers fidgeting with the fabric. I want to say more, to make her believe me, but my phone buzzes on the nightstand—a reminder that the car taking me to the airport will be here any minute.

Reluctantly, I stand to get dressed, each movement feeling heavier than it should.

As I pull my shirt over my head, I glance back at her. She's still sitting there, her legs tucked under her, the faintest smile tugging at her lips despite the tension in the room. I hesitate for a moment, then ask, "Do you have plans for St. Patrick's Day?"

Her head tilts as she releases a quick laugh. "St. Patrick's Day? That's random."

I shrug, keeping my tone light even as the fear of losing her before I've truly had a chance settles heavy in my chest, my heartbeat slipping out of rhythm. "Not really. It's in a month, and I happen to know a great pub that does it right. You should come visit."

Her smile falters, and she shakes her head slightly. "Archie..."

"Don't," I interrupt gently, stepping closer to the bed. "Don't say no before you've thought about it. I'll cover the cost—plane ticket, everything. Just come. We'll figure the rest out later. But I can't leave here without you knowing how much I want to see you again."

Her eyes search mine, and for a moment, I'm terrified she's going to refuse. Then, slowly, she exhales and looks away, a small grin forming on her lips. "You're relentless, you know that?"

"Maybe," I admit, crouching down in front of her so we're eye to eye. "But only because I think this—*us*—is worth it. Don't you?"

She bites her lip, her gaze softening as it locks onto mine. "I think it might be," she whispers, barely audible.

"Good." I reach for her hand, my thumb brushing over her knuckles. "Then let me prove it to you."

She doesn't respond right away, but the doubt in her eyes fades as she gives me a small nod. "Alright," she says quietly. "I'll think about it."

"That's all I'm asking." I rise to my feet and brush a kiss to her forehead. "But I'm holding you to it."

She laughs again, this time a little brighter, and as I finish getting ready, the weight in the room lifts. By the time I turn back to her, there's a spark of optimism in her expression that mirrors my own.

"See you soon?" I ask, hovering above her lips before giving her one last lingering kiss.

Her hazy green eyes meet mine. "Yes," she says with a shy smile. "See you soon."

I leave her apartment with a sense of hope. Whatever happens, I know this isn't the end. Not by a long shot.

CHAPTER 17

Hillary

TAKE THE LEAP

THEN

"What is the emergency?" Marisa demands as she barrels through the front door of my apartment. "I got here as fast as I could."

Judging by the wild look in her eyes and the way her hair is half falling out of whatever rushed attempt at a bun she'd thrown it into, I probably shouldn't have texted her *SOS. Emergency. Come ASAP.*

I can see how she might've assumed the situation was life-or-death.

Instead, it's just me losing my ever-loving mind.

After I catch her up on the Archie situation, she just stares at me, jaw practically on the floor.

It's not like this is coming out of nowhere. I already told her about London. I told her he was coming to Seattle. Logically, the fact that we slept together shouldn't be all that shocking.

And yet, based on her expression, you'd think I'd just confessed we got married instead.

"You mean to tell me the hot ginger you haven't shut up about since you got back dicked you down so well you're walking around looking starry-eyed, and not only that, he invited you to London on an all-expenses-paid trip, and you're what...confused?" She throws her hands in the air. "There is nothing to be confused about. You are going on that trip. I don't care if I have to physically drag you onto the plane myself. You're going."

I draw my knees to my chest and rest my chin against my thigh. From the moment Archie and I said our goodbyes, there's been this hollow ache inside me. I actually cried after he left.

Cried.

I barely know him.

Sure, the chemistry between us is unlike anything I've ever experienced, and the sex is...well, it's phenomenal. But I don't even know his favorite color. I don't know what kind of music he listens to. Does he watch sports? Does he have some obscure hobby he's obsessed with? I know the way his lips feel against mine. The way my heart flutters when our eyes meet. The way he looks at me like I'm the only person in the room. But beyond that? Nothing.

I shouldn't feel this attached. And I definitely shouldn't waste my time investing in anything more than a few fun days with a man who lives thousands of miles away.

We could never work.

It's the definition of unrealistic.

"I can't go," I tell Marisa, unable to hide the defeat in my voice. "What's the point? We live so far apart I don't even know what time it is there. We could never work."

She rolls her eyes. "You know what I hear? A bunch of excuses."

"I'm being practical. And I can't jump from one relationship to another."

"Says who? This guy could be the one, the man of your dreams! And you're going to pass him up because of a few obstacles. I didn't realize you were such a quitter."

She's baiting me. I know this, but I'm still letting it get to me.

"You're forgetting one of those obstacles is the Atlantic Ocean."

"Hill." Her tone turns serious. "Sometimes you need to take the leap, jump without knowing where you'll end up. How many opportunities are you going to get for a literal British knight in shining armor to sweep you off your feet? If anything, do it for the story. Do it for the plot. But don't let fear—or that shithead Kyle—rob you of taking chances just because they're scary."

Her words sit with me long after she leaves. And later that evening, as I'm getting ready for bed, my phone buzzes, alerting me to a text from Archie.

ARCHIE

Finally landed in London. Is it coming on too strong if I tell you I've been missing you since we parted ways?

A rush of tingles zings up my spine, and I can hardly contain my smile.

I'm glad you made it safely. And it's definitely not coming on too strong, because I've been missing you too.

I wouldn't normally be so honest, but as much as I hate to admit it, Marisa is right. Sometimes you need to take a chance. And something deep in my gut is telling me it might be the chance of a lifetime.

ARCHIE

> Glad to hear it, love. I'm a walking zombie
> and need to grab a cab to get home. Would
> it be alright if I called you tomorrow? Not
> sure I'll last much longer without hearing
> your voice.

A squeal slips out before I can stop it, and I hide my face in my hands, dizzy with giddy delight. The speed at which I'm falling for Archie should be studied. I've never been the kick-my-feet-and-giggle type, but he's turned me into exactly that.

> I would love that. Get home safely and get
> some rest!

I fall asleep smiling like a fool, a swarm of butterflies in my stomach and the faintest twinge of worry that I'm setting myself up for heartbreak.

THE NEXT DAY — 9:12 A.M. (SEATTLE) / 5:12 P.M. (LONDON)

My phone rings with Archie's name lighting up the screen.

I answer instantly.

"Hi," I say, failing miserably at playing it cool.

"Hi." His voice pours through the speaker, his accent so soothing and sexy I have to bite my lip to keep from moaning. Archie's voice was already melt-worthy. But through the phone, it's downright dangerous. Panty-ruining dangerous. "Is it too early? I triple-checked the time before calling."

"No." I smile. "I've been up for a few hours. Just got to work, actually."

He hums thoughtfully. "I can call back if it's a bad time."

"No!" I say too quickly, laughing when I realize I have no chill with this man. "Now is perfect."

I can't see it, but I feel his grin through the line.

"It's very rude of the universe to allow our paths to cross, leaving us to figure out how to handle how much we can't stop thinking about each other."

"We?" I tease. "Pretty confident there, aren't you?"

"Most would say wildly delusional. But confident works too."

My pulse quickens, a girlish giggle slipping free. "Well, don't be too hard on yourself. I'd say whatever is happening here is definitely mutual."

"Good." He laughs through an exhale.

I sink further into my office chair, sporting a cheek-splitting smile.

We talk for forty-five minutes about nothing and everything.

His favorite color is green. "Like my eyes?" I joke.

"Precisely that shade," he replies.

He plays five-a-side football on Sundays. And it's embarrassing it took me at least a solid minute to figure out he's referring to soccer.

He enjoys boxing, which explains why he was able to throw such a good punch.

He tells me he can't stand reality TV, but I think I could convert him.

He likes a variety of music but is currently fixated on The 1975. I tell him I'll report back on my thoughts after I give them a listen.

A few hours later, he sends me a picture of the pub midshift, captioned: Your seat is empty.

And just like that, I decide falling for Archie is going to be the easy part. It's everything that comes after that terrifies me.

WEEK ONE

ARCHIE

I'm glad we did lots of sightseeing while
you were here.

Why's that?

ARCHIE

Because, hypothetically, if you come for St.
Patrick's Day, I won't feel guilty.

Guilty over what?

ARCHIE

Keeping you in bed.

"Well, aren't you glowing," my mom says, standing in the doorway of my office.

I slam my phone down, face hot with embarrassment.

"Talking to Prince Charming, I take it?"

Laughing, I shake my head. "What gave me away?"

She settles into the chair across from my desk. "Oh, just that goofy look on your face."

"Archie is..." I trail off, unable to put into words just how much he's come to mean to me in such a short amount of time.

"I get it." She smiles gently. "I was the same way with your dad. I'm not sure I've ever seen you quite so smitten."

"I—I don't really know where it's going. We haven't put a label on it. It's all very new."

"You'll figure it out." She says it so matter-of-factly, I wish

I had an ounce of the confidence she seems to feel for the situation.

As I shoot off emails and follow up with a few developers I've been waiting to hear from, my mind continues to drift back to Archie and his invitation to visit.

Of course I want to see him again. That's not the issue. The issue is I know if I go, my feelings are only going to get stronger, and part of me wants to protect myself from letting it get that far.

Getting over someone terrible, like Kyle, is much easier than trying to get over someone amazing.

But everything in me is screaming to say yes. And it's too loud to ignore.

I quickly check the time to make sure it's not too late. Thankfully it's only eight in the evening in London.

> Hypothetically, if I visit, what hotel would you recommend?

Instead of texting me back, he calls.

"Hello?" I answer, feigning innocence.

"It's cute that you think I would have you stay in a hotel room. As if I could let you out of my sight while we're in the same city. If you'd prefer to stay in a hotel, then I'm afraid I'll have to join you."

"What about Emma? Not that I don't want to see her, but I think we might need some privacy."

My face heats up a few degrees just thinking about being alone with Archie again. I have a feeling I only got a small glimpse of what he's capable of in bed. I'll need to sleep with him at least a couple more times to be sure. For science, of course.

He's quiet for a stretch too long, and I swallow down the lump of nerves in my throat.

"Does this mean you're actually coming?" he asks quietly.

"If you'll have me," I whisper, holding my breath.

He lets out a rush of air through a sigh. "You have no idea how happy that makes me, love. And Emma can stay with her friends or our parents, or we can stay in a hotel. I honestly don't care as long as I get to see you."

Moisture stings behind my eyes. The happy kind. The I-can't-believe-I'm-really-doing-this kind. "I can't wait."

Week Two

We fall into a rhythm.

Good morning texts from him are my goodnight texts.

Voice notes. FaceTime chats. Sending random videos on social media.

One night I'm tossing and turning at three in the morning, unable to fall asleep.

I know he's probably at work, but I text him anyway.

You busy?

ARCHIE

Just got home. Work was slow.

I can't sleep…

He FaceTimes me, and though I'm sure I look terrible, I'm hoping the darkness of my bedroom conceals most of my flaws because I'm not passing up a chance to talk to him. Even if it's only for five minutes.

His face fills the screen of my phone and my heart jumps to life.

"Why can't you sleep?" he asks, concerned.

I shrug, resting my cheek on my pillow. "I'm not sure. Can't stop thinking. Can't get comfortable. It's just one of those nights."

"What can I do?"

"Nothing, I guess." I laugh quietly. "What would you do if you were with me?"

It's definitely a question that's pushing in a certain direction, but maybe that's exactly what I need.

He looks around, like he's checking to make sure he's alone. "I'd eat your pussy."

"Archie!" I nearly shout. His dirty talk sounds a million times more filthy paired with his accent. And it drives me wild.

"What?" He smirks. "I would. First, I'd lick your clit, a few slow flicks, right before burying my tongue in your sweet little cunt."

My eyes roll back, a whimpering groan clawing up my throat as I press my thighs together.

"Then what?" I ask, so breathless I'd be embarrassed if I wasn't so turned on.

He starts moving through his flat, and I hear the soft thud of a door closing. "Touch yourself, love. And show me," he says as he gets situated on his bed.

I've never had phone sex. In fact, I've always thought it was kind of cheesy. How can two people actually be turned on when they're not in the same room?

But now, I take back every opinion I've ever had on the matter. I am absolutely turned on. So much so I don't hesitate to slip off my pajama shorts and slide my hand inside my underwear.

"Are you touching yourself?" Archie asks, voice strained.

I nod, my back arching slightly as I dip a finger inside my wet center.

"Yes."

"Prop the phone up on a pillow. I need to see you."

"You first." I challenge.

Within seconds, more of him comes into view. He's sitting up, back against his headboard, slacks unbuttoned, shirt collar loose, sleeves rolled up and showing off his muscular forearms.

God, I wish I could touch him.

"Are we doing this together or are you just a spectator?" I ask before biting my lip to contain my nervous smile.

"I'll do whatever you want if it means I get to watch you get off."

The way he's looking at me, a mix of desperation and adoration, gives me a surge of boldness I don't normally possess.

"Take your cock out. And stroke it."

He listens to my instructions, his hardened cock springing free, his hand wrapping around it.

I'd forgotten how big it is, and an ache starts to build, one only he can fill.

My mouth salivates when I notice the head of his cock is moistened at the tip, pre-cum I'd gladly lick if I were with him.

"Show me, Hillary," he moans. "Spread your legs and let me see how wet that perfect pussy is for me. Please, love."

I do as he asks, positioning my phone and parting my legs to give him the view he wants.

I can't recall anyone ever begging me, ever being so obviously desperate for me, and it's only making me wetter, needier.

The satisfied groan he releases ripples over me like a wave.

"Fuuuuuck," he drags as he pumps his cock.

I nearly melt on the spot, nothing but a useless puddle of lust.

"Take off your shirt." His voice is a rasp that sets off a chain reaction in my body.

Quickly, I strip off my top and toss it aside. As one hand

rubs at my pussy, the other toys with my nipples, imagining it's Archie touching me this way.

"Yes, love. Just like that. Keep touching yourself. You are... fuck." His eyes are wide as they trail over my body. "You're so fucking beautiful, so sexy I might never recover from the pleasure of seeing you like this."

"Archie," I beg, but I'm not sure what I'm begging for. Him? Relief? Relief only he can provide? It's everything.

"Add another finger. I know you can take it."

I add another, relishing in the stretch around it.

My hips buck of their own accord, chasing my orgasm.

I'm not sure what it says about me that only a few weeks ago this man was punching my ex-boyfriend, nearly a complete stranger, and now I'm splayed out naked, spread-eagle for him—and I've never felt more powerful.

We come together, our groans and sighs tangling over one another. He gathers his cum in a tissue while my drenched fingers remain between my thighs.

"I wish you weren't so far away," he says quietly after we've both come down from the high.

"Me too." My voice is low, sadness mixed with sudden exhaustion hitting me.

"Get some sleep, love."

Week Three

ARCHIE

Have I mentioned how much I miss you?

Only every day.

ARCHIE

Is it annoying you yet?

No, so please never stop telling me.

"So you're really going to London?" Marisa asks, tucking her legs beneath her on my couch during our girls' night before taking a sip of wine. She grimaces and sets the glass down. "Not sure I'll ever become a wine drinker."

I laugh and take a drink. It's a cheap bottle, so it doesn't go down very smoothly. "I'm really going."

I honestly can't believe it myself. If someone had told me a month ago I'd be flying halfway across the world to visit a guy I spent less than seventy-two hours with, I'd never have believed them. But as odd as it is, Archie doesn't feel like a stranger to me. I'm not sure he ever did. There's just been something about him from the beginning that felt familiar, some instinct in me that told me he was one of the good ones.

"I'm proud of you," Marisa says, a wide smile across her face. "It's already one of the best love stories I've ever heard, and it's just the beginning."

"Let's not get ahead of ourselves. Love is a bit of a stretch. We're just two people who enjoy each other's company, and we happen to live in two different countries."

She blows out a puff of air. "Sure, Hill. Sure. Keep telling yourself that. We both know you're head over heels for this guy, and when you get back from London you're going to be full-on in love with him. Assuming you come back at all."

"I'm coming back. My life is here."

"Whatever you say." Her tone is dripping with disbelief.

It's one of those things I've tried not to think about too much. If whatever is happening between me and Archie continues, one of us will have to move. And that's a very big decision to make. It's a life-changing one.

THREE WEEKS, FIVE DAYS BEFORE ST. PATRICK'S DAY

ARCHIE

I'm counting down the days.

Me too. These next couple days are going to be torture.

ARCHIE

Any requests? Anywhere you want eat?
Places you'd like to see?

I only care about seeing you.

CHAPTER 18

Archie

MIGHT NOT LET HER GO

Then

"You're going to sweat through your shirt," Will tells me, not helping to ease my nerves whatsoever.

I roll my eyes. "Remind me again why I brought you?"

He claps my back a little harder than necessary. "So you two lovebirds can makeout in the back seat."

"We're not going to makeout. We're adults. We can wait until you're lurking eyes aren't anywhere in sight."

I flick my wrist again, checking my watch for the tenth time, as if the clock is suddenly going to speed up. Hillary and I have spoken every day since she left, and it didn't take me long at all to realize it's far from enough. I cannot wait to have her in my arms, and this time I might not let her go.

Her plane landed about twenty minutes ago, so she should be making it to baggage claim shortly.

"Ope," Will sounds. "I think I've spotted her."

Sure enough, I see a mass of blonde curls in the distance and my heart kicks into gear. Without wasting another second,

I'm moving forward, bypassing the crowd, not taking my eyes off her.

She smiles when she sees me, drops her bags, and sprints toward me.

I catch her, lifting her off the ground, her legs winding around my waist, arms circling my neck, scent enveloping me.

And just like that, I can breathe again.

"Holy shit I missed you," her muffled voice says into my neck.

"You have no idea."

Her gaze connects with mine, and even though she looks tired from a long day of traveling, she's still so fucking stunning.

Our lips crash in a frenzy, starved for one another. My tongue slips in, causing a moan to vibrate out of her that makes me wish we were alone. I'd love nothing more than to strip her bare and sink inside her.

"Mm." She breaks our kiss, lips swollen and perfectly ravaged. "How far is the flat from here?" Her skin pinkens, eyes bright.

"Far enough we'll have to restrain ourselves a while longer."

She gives Will a hug when she sees him and for a brief moment I'm irrationally jealous of my married brother respectfully hugging my girl.

Hillary happily chats with me and Will during the ride, and while the conversation is pleasant and innocent, I haven't stopped touching her. Stoking my thumb along her wrist, sliding my arm around her, skimming the sliver of skin at the hem of her top. I can't stop touching her. I may never stop.

Will pulls up to the curb. "Alright we're here." His eyes find mine, a mischievous grin on his face. "Don't do anything I wouldn't do."

Will was the troublemaker of us three, so I know exactly what he's trying to say.

"Bye, Will." Hillary waves as he drives off.

Once his car is out of sight, I find Hillary staring at the pub with a confused expression.

"What's wrong, love?"

"Why is the pub closed?"

I grab her suitcase with one hand and reach my other out to grab hers. "Sunday. We're closed on Sundays."

"Oh," she drags. "So we're all alone?"

Guiding her toward the door, I nod. "Mm-hmm. I had to bribe Emma—lent her my car to make herself scarce—but she insisted on coming to see you before you leave."

"Well I'd love to see her, but right now I'm very happy to just have you to myself."

Once I get the door unlocked and her stuff safely inside, Hillary wanders over to the barstool she sat it when we first met, running her hand along the leather back.

"So weird how much has changed since the last time I was here."

"Kind of wild to think about," I say, coming up behind her and circling my arms around her waist, pulling her gently into me.

Her body relaxes against mine, a contented hum passing between her lips.

And I realize this is exactly where I'm meant to be. Wherever she is, that's where I belong, because I've never felt at home in another person before. Hillary is home—not any home I've ever known, but the one I've unknowingly been searching for, only recognizing it once she was in my arms.

"Shall we head up?" I say after a long moment.

She nods against my chest, and we slowly make our way upstairs.

I roll her suitcase into the living room and then clap my hands together, nerves bundling within me.

I wanted her here so badly, and now that she is, it feels like everything inside me has gone quiet. Like my world narrowed just to her.

She watches me with that soft, knowing smile. "Why do you look nervous?"

"I'm not nervous."

"You are." She steps closer. "You're doing this ticking thing with your jaw."

I huff a laugh. "I am not doing a ticking thing with my jaw."

"You absolutely are."

She closes the distance between us, sliding her hands up my chest, fingers curling into my shirt like she needs me to steady herself.

The thought alone makes something sharp and protective bloom in my chest.

"I just..." I drag a hand through my hair. "I've been thinking about this moment for weeks. And now you're here and it feels big."

Her expression eases, eyes wide and clear. "It is big," she whispers.

I cup her face, thumbs brushing over her cheeks. She melts into me and it feels like an honor to be able to touch her like this after not being able to for so long.

"I don't want this to be just a visit," I say quietly.

Her breath catches in her throat. "Archie..."

"No, let me say it." My forehead presses to hers. "I've tried to play it cool. But I'm not capable of it. I've tried to pretend this is just casual, that we're just two people having a nice little international fling." I let out a humorless laugh. "But it's not that. Not for me."

Her hands tighten on my shirt despite the flash of hesitancy in her gaze.

"I don't want anyone else," I continue. "I don't even see anyone else. I'm not interested in anyone else. I want you. Properly. Fully. However far that goes."

"You're saying..." she swallows. "You want this to be exclusive?"

"Yes, I'm saying I want you to myself. So if there's another guy in the picture back home, lose him. If we're doing this, we're doing it right. No maybes. No halfway."

There's a beat of silence where everything hangs between us—fear, hope, the fucking Atlantic Ocean.

"There's nobody else. I don't want anyone but you," she admits softly.

The relief that floods me is almost dizzying.

I kiss her then. Slow, savoring her. Not frantic like the airport. Not desperate like we're trying to make up for lost time. It's the kind of kiss I could do for the rest of my life.

Her fingers slide into my hair, and I walk her backward to the couch. She laughs softly as she falls onto it, tugging me down with her.

My hands map her slowly—waist, hips, the curve of her thigh—reacquainting myself with the feel of her. She sighs into my mouth, arching into me, and the sound alone nearly undoes me.

"I needed this," she breathes. "You."

"Me too." I kiss the corner of her mouth.

Her hands slide beneath my shirt, palms warm against my skin. We move together instinctively, like the weeks apart never happened.

But eventually she stills, hand running the length of my spine in a delicate caress.

"Okay," she says softly, brushing her thumb over my jaw. "If we're doing this. If we're exclusive...how?"

The question lands like being doused in cold water.

I lean back slightly so I can see her face.

"We figure it out."

"That's not a plan."

"It's a start." I exhale. "We talk every day already. That doesn't change. We visit. We save. We look at jobs. We see what's possible."

She studies me carefully, gnawing on her bottom lip. "You'd move?"

"If that's what it takes." My answer is immediate because it was never out of the question. "Or you move. Or we pick somewhere new. I don't care where I am as long as I'm with you."

I'd leave this flat. I'd leave the pub. I'd leave my country. I'd rebuild from scratch if it meant waking up next to her every day.

"I don't want to lose you because it's complicated," I continue. "Distance is hard. Time zones are hard. But not having you at all? That would be exponentially worse."

Her eyes shine, unshed tears balancing on the edge.

"I don't know what to say. You're serious?" she whispers.

"I've never been more serious about anything."

She pulls me down into another kiss—slower this time, softer, but deeper somehow. Like sealing something sacred.

When we finally separate, she presses her forehead to mine.

"Okay," she says, voice trembling. "Let's do this. For real."

"For real," I echo.

Hillary insisted on showering before anything physical could continue. I told her I didn't mind one bit, yet it did nothing to convince her.

But knowing she's wet and naked, with only a door between us, is a special kind of torture.

I pace once across the living room. Then back again.

The sound of the shower running is a steady reminder she's really here. In my flat. Under my roof. Steam curling around skin I've memorized in fragments and flashes and late-night fantasies.

I rake a hand through my hair as the pipes groan when she turns the water off, and I freeze mid-step.

The bathroom door clicks open.

"Archie?"

Her voice is a beautiful melody drifting down the hallway. I'm moving before I can stop myself.

She's standing with the door swung open, steam clouding around her, wrapped in one of my towels. Her damp curls cling to her shoulders, skin flushed from the heat of the shower.

I actually forget how to breathe.

"Is everything okay? You don't look well," she teases, a mischievous grin on her lips. This woman knows exactly what she's doing to me.

And fuck if it isn't sexy.

Water droplets fall down the curve of her neck. On instinct, I lift my hand and follow one with my thumb, satisfied at the goosebumps that rise on her skin in a trail from my touch.

"That feels good," she whispers, eyes falling shut.

"Good." My hand settles at her waist, fingers pressing into warm skin beneath the towel. She exhales slowly, lips parting.

I kiss her. My hand slides to the back of her neck, tilting her head so I can deepen it. She tastes like mint toothpaste and something distinctly her.

My mouth drifts from her lips to her jaw, to the sensitive

spot just below her ear. She sucks in a breath, hands tightening.

"Archie," she sighs.

"Yes, love?"

The towel loosens, slipping slightly. I pause, giving her the chance to stop me.

She doesn't.

Instead, she reaches for the hem of my shirt and pulls it over my head. The moment I'm free of it, I give her towel a tug and watch it slip from her body and pool at her feet.

We reach for each other, our bodies clicking into place like a piece that was once whole.

The contact of her bare skin against mine is electric. Weeks of distance dissolve in a second.

I guide her backward toward the bed, our steps clumsy and uncoordinated because neither of us wants to break contact long enough to see where we're going.

She falls onto it with a soft laugh, pulling me down with her.

I hover over her for a moment, taking her in.

"I know this is way too soon and way too fast, but I'm falling hard, love. In fact, I might already be there."

She reaches up, cradling my face. "I'm falling fast too. This is insane, isn't it?"

I capture her lips with mine. "Ridiculous."

She laughs against my mouth. "We've obviously lost our minds."

I let out a hungry sound when she nips at my lip. "Absolutely."

I kiss her again, slower this time. My hands trace familiar paths—her waist, the curve of her hip, the line of her thigh—relearning her. She arches into me, breath hitching, and I have to close my eyes for a second just to steady myself.

Between the heat and the urgency and the want, I'm not sure where I end and she begins.

She strokes my cock over the fabric of my pants. "Condom," she says into my mouth. "I can't wait. I need you."

In record time, my pants are off, and together we're rolling a condom over my achingly hard length.

I slide inside her like we've done this thousands of times. Maybe in this lifetime we're just beginning, but something about us feels inevitable. Like she's been mine in every existence. My body knows hers instinctively. I'm attuned to her in a way I've never been with anyone else.

Things turn urgent quickly. I palm under her thigh, lifting it to go deeper, pressing her further into the mattress. I kiss her neck as I thrust in and out of her, taking her as deep and as hard as she can handle.

She's gasping and cursing, praising a god nowhere in the room with us. It's just me, driving her into oblivion. My vision fades to black, waves of euphoria crashing over me—overwhelming and wonderful.

Her nails claw at my back, her heels digging into me, her head thrown back in ecstasy.

"You take me so well, love." I thrust harder. "Made for me."

"Yes," she moans. "So fucking good."

I'm going to come soon. It's a battle of restraint and pleasure to hold back and make sure she's with me.

Reaching between us, I circle her clit, giving her what she needs to send her over the edge.

Her legs start shaking, her pussy pulsing around my cock, drawing out my own orgasm. We come together, a flurry of satisfied groans bouncing between us.

Neither one of us moves, remaining intertwined. My cock slowly softens inside her, but I have no desire to break our connection.

"You're going to blow up my whole life, aren't you?" Hillary's hushed voice says after a while, a sated smile across her face.

"Something like that." I plant featherlight kisses over her collarbone, down to the swell of her breast. "I think everything is about to change."

Hillary's visit is entirely too short.

We make it to the St. Patrick's Day celebration at the pub, the place bursting at the seams with green and too much alcohol. Emma joins us, stealing Hillary's attention for most of the festivities, the two of them already thick as thieves.

Later that evening, when the pub empties and the city settles, we retreat upstairs.

We stay wrapped around each other, tangled in my bedsheets, limbs intertwined like we're trying to memorize the shape of one another. We talk about possibilities that feel both impossibly far away and suddenly within reach. We sketch out the beginnings of a future, the kind you're almost afraid to say too loudly in case the universe hears and decides to put every obstacle in your way.

I can't predict what's coming.

I don't know if I'll be lucky enough to spend my life with someone as extraordinary as Hillary.

But I know this: I'll try my damnedest to keep her. To make her happy. To build something strong enough to survive oceans and doubt and whatever else could keep us apart.

Because she already feels like the best decision I've ever made.

CHAPTER 19

Hillary

LAST CALL

Now

As we pull up to our house, a rush of excitement fills my chest. I can't wait to see Josephine again. Our weekend away at Red Mountain was everything we needed, but I'm ready to be back to our regular life with our baby girl in my arms.

Archie parks the car, and as soon as I step out, I turn to him, a smile breaking across my face. "Thanks for this weekend, daddy." I give him a wink and watch as my naughty little word unravels him.

"Love, you can't say things like that when I won't get you to myself for hours."

I giggle. "Or you could just meet me in the shower after I get some cuddles in. Your mom can watch her while we *unpack*."

He breathes a laugh as his skin flushes. "You're so naughty," he whispers.

Our short weekend away reminded me of something. I can't let motherhood consume me to the point that I forget about myself and the needs and desires I have. I want to find away to incorporate us into our daily lives.

As we walk into the house, the familiar comfort of our home immediately envelops me. It's quieter than usual, and I glance at Archie, my excitement mounting.

"Do you think she's awake?" I ask, trying to listen for the sounds of our daughter and Joanna.

"I'll check," he replies, moving toward the living room.

I follow closely behind, my heart racing with anticipation.

When we reach the living room, I spot Josephine in her playpen, her big blue eyes blinking at us in surprise. She squeals, her little hands reaching out for me. I scoop her up, feeling her warmth against my chest, and I can't help but shower her with kisses.

"I missed you so much, sweet girl!" I say, my voice muffled against her soft hair. Her laughter fills the room, and for a moment, I lose myself in the joy of being reunited, inhaling her baby scent and tickling my nose with her red curls.

Archie watches us, leaning against the doorframe with a tender smile on his face. It's moments like this that make my heart swell. I catch his eye, grateful for the time we had together but even more grateful that we're home and back together as a family.

Once I set Josephine down, she starts to wiggle in excitement. I laugh, watching as she reaches for her toys and then turns to Archie. "Did you have a good time with Gran?"

Archie scoops her up, showering her with even more kisses. "She spoiled her rotten," Archie replies with a playful grin. "Did she give you any trouble?" Archie asks Joanna, who's peeling potatoes in the kitchen.

"Never," Joanna replies. "Perfect angel, unlike you at that age. I ever tell you what a terror he was, hon?" Joanna tells me, laughing to herself.

"No, but tell me more. Gotta be prepared for the next kid."

"Pregnant already?" Joanna jokes.

I shake my head and meet Archie's gaze. "Not yet, not for a while. But eventually we want at least one more."

"I like threes myself," Joanna says, unaware that her son is undressing me with his eyes from across the room. He sets Josephine back in her playpen and raises his brows at me. "Three is a lucky number, you know?"

"Mum," Archie croaks. "We're going to unpack and freshen up. Mind watching Jojo for a bit longer?"

She waves us off. "Go for it. I'm making cottage pie for dinner. Should be done in about an hour."

"Okay," Archie calls out, dragging me up the stairs. "We'll be back down in an hour."

"You think she knows?" I whisper as Archie hauls me into the bathroom.

"Who cares," he mumbles against my neck as he tugs at my clothes.

We have a very nice, very long shower, and then join Joanna and Josephine for dinner.

After dinner, we send Joanna up to her room, not letting her both cook and clean for us tonight after she already did so much over the weekend. Archie bounces Josephine around the kitchen while I dry off the last of the dishes.

"I think someone is ready for her nighttime bottle," Archie tells Josephine in his baby voice reserved only for her.

"I'll make it," I tell him.

He waves me off. "I got it. Go lie down and relax."

My instinct is to brush him off, but I fight it. I need to learn to accept his help and stop taking on every little thing. So I do.

Upstairs, I run through my evening routine, and just as

I'm sinking into the familiar comfort of our bed, Archie walks with Josephine cradled on his hip.

Once he gets her settled in her basinet, he crawls into bed with me and hands me a glass of whiskey I hadn't noticed was sitting on his nightstand.

"What's this?"

"Last call, love. Thought I'd make you a drink before we shut down for the night."

"Oh, really?" I laugh. "I didn't realize our kitchen has closing hours."

Archie chuckles, his arm wrapping around my shoulders as he nestles close. "Every good establishment does, right? But for you," he murmurs, brushing a soft kiss to my forehead. "There is no last call."

I smile, feeling the warmth of the whiskey settle in my chest. The quiet of the house surrounds us, and for a moment, all I hear is the faint melody of the lullaby from Josephine's mobile and the rhythm of Archie's breathing beside me. It's peaceful, grounding—a perfect ending to a weekend that reminded me just how much we need these moments to recharge, to reconnect.

Taking a sip, I curl up against him. "Thank you for this," I whisper. "For the weekend, for everything. It's easy to get lost in our busy schedules and structured routines."

Archie pulls me closer, his hand tracing soothing circles along my arm. "You deserve it, love. And we'll keep finding ways to make time for each other—no matter how crazy things get."

I nod, letting the silence settle around us. As tired as I am, I fight the sleep trying to take over, not wanting tomorrow to come just yet. It's these small rituals, these little gestures, that fill my heart and remind me why we work so hard, why we juggle and compromise and grow.

When I finally set my empty glass on the bedside table,

Archie leans over, a mischievous glint in his eyes. "So, love, any last requests before the night officially ends?"

I smirk, pulling him down beside me. "Just one." I press my lips to his, savoring the warmth of his touch. Of all the pubs in all of London, I had to walk into his brother's—and lose my heart to the handsome bartender behind the bar. In that twist of fate, we found where we truly belong—together, making the most of our last call and every new beginning that follows.

Do you want to stay up to date with the rest of the Red Mountain crew? Scan the QR code below to sign up for my newsletter, where I'll be sharing exclusive updates on the Red Mountain Series and future projects.

Want to chat all things Last Call and the Red Mountain Series? Consider joining my Facebook Reader Group. Scan the QR code below for unhinged commentary, bonus content, and exclusive sneak peeks.

First and foremost, I want to thank my readers! Your love for *Rare Blend* made this novella possible. It was such a joy to dive back into the Red Mountain universe through fresh eyes and to get a glimpse of the Ledger family from an outsider's perspective.

To Lucy, thank you for all of your British insight. I felt so out of my element, and I can't thank you enough for answering all my questions. You truly helped me bring Archie to life.

To my beta babes—Rose, Sydney, Rachel, Madeline, and Shelbie, thank you for taking the time to read this story and give me the feedback I needed to make it what it is today. And Shelbie, just know you were the flame that lit the fire—*Last Call* wouldn't exist without you.

To my Grandma Lillie, you've been gone for a while now, but you never let me forget that my roots are British. Not royal, unfortunately—that's a bummer. Paid the money, took the test, and it turns out we came from peasants. Alas, I'll keep holding out hope for the day someone shows up at my door claiming I'm the Princess of Genovia.

To my editor, Andrea, Endless thanks for never telling me no and for letting me treat deadlines like rough targets. Surely, I'm your problem child client.

To my husband, I didn't really tell you much about this project, but you saw me typing away and kept me fueled with warm beverages to help me keep going.

To Litzuli, my platonic soulmate, I tell you everything, and you always listen, always support me, and always believe in me. Having you in my corner keeps me going, even when I feel like giving up.

Lastly, to anyone who has ever been in or is currently in an abusive relationship, it can happen to anyone, and it does happen to anyone. Abuse doesn't discriminate. You're not alone. Seek help, get help, and never stop fighting for yourself. Your life matters.

If you or someone you know is experiencing domestic abuse, please know that you are not alone. There is help available. The National Domestic Violence Hotline offers confidential support 24/7 at 1-800-799-SAFE (7233) or via their website at thehotline.org. Remember, reaching out for support is a brave and powerful step. You deserve to feel safe and supported.

Technical writer turned romance author Michelle Naomi Mosley writes small town romances with relatable characters and heartfelt narratives, incorporating humor and open-door spice in all her stories.

Michelle lives in Washington State's wine country with her husband. When she's not writing, she's reading, cooking the latest viral recipe, or redecorating her home for the millionth time. Since deciding to take the plunge and finally make her writing dreams a reality, it's been a whirlwind of late nights crafting stories and trying to keep up with the countless book ideas that strike her at any given moment.

You can follow her on Instagram and most socials @authormichellenaomimosley. For more information on books, merchandise, and newsletter sign-ups, visit authormichellenaomimosley.com.